GRAMPA'S
ALKALI

Jo Bannatyne-Cugnet

Red Deer College Press

3rd Printing, 1999

Northern Lights Young Novels are published by
Red Deer College Press
56 Avenue & 32 Street Box 5005
Red Deer Alberta Canada T4N 5H5

Edited for the Press by Tim Wynne-Jones.
Cover art by Yvette Moore.
Cover design by Christine Toller.
Text design by Dennis Johnson.
Printed and bound in Canada by Friesen Corp.
Red Deer College Press.
The publishers gratefully acknowledge the financial assistance of the Alberta Foundation for the Arts, the Canada Council, the Department of Communications and Red Deer College.

Canadian Cataloguing in Publication Data
Bannatyne-Cugnet, Jo
Alkali
(Northern lights young novels)
ISBN 0-88995-096-2
I. Title. II. Series.
PS8553.A56A72 1993
jC813'.54   C92-091842-5
PZ7.B36A1 1993

To my son Dan, who asked,
"Why can't a kid on the prairies be a hero?"
–J. B-C.

GRAMPA'S ALKALI

CHAPTER
ONE

Alkali sat in the shelterbelt, a thick, twisted hedge of caragana trees restrained by a barbwire fence. It almost surrounded the entire farmstead, the only defense against the constant barrage of wind that sweeps the prairies. In the winter it held large snowdrifts, the closest thing to a hill for tobogganing; and in the summer it held drifting topsoil. But for Alkali the shelterbelt provided a cave. It wasn't a real cave like you'd find in a mountain. Someday, he would have the real thing, but for now this made do. Normally, caraganas are impenetrable. For Alkali the small enclosure had always been there. It had never occurred to him that perhaps long ago a previous tenant—another small boy—had carved out this secret place in a younger hedge.

The cave was spacious. He had to crouch at the entrance, but once inside he could stand up straight. Alkali had furnished the inside with a couch fashioned from bales of straw. Two blocks cut from a blackened railway tie served as stools. Boards propped in the caragana branches held his treasures—a genuine lava rock, chunks of petrified wood and several old Black Cat tobacco tins filled with an assortment of spent shotgun shells, various sizes of ball bearings and arrowhead flint. It was the perfect place for Alkali, more perfect in summer of course, because thousands of tiny caragana leaves camouflaged his hideout. And the location was ideal. From here he could survey his entire kingdom: his house, his grandparents' house, the chicken coop, the barn. The workshop.

Alkali sat running his fingers over his latest find—a garter snake skin. He had found it in his mother's petunia bed by the back step. She had said, "Find the snake it belongs to and burn them both!" Alkali had set about searching for the snake with no intention of killing it. So far he hadn't found it. He was grateful for its skin. He held it up to a ray of sunlight. It measured from his thumb to his elbow. The scaly skin was like a series of tiny, dirty windows joined together.

He wondered if it had hurt to shed this skin.

He was distracted by the sound of the garden tractor starting up in the workshop across the yard. His mouth said "No!" but he didn't hear the word. A thunderous crash from the workshop drowned out all sound. Alkali froze. It seemed to him that everything in the world had stopped except that noise, which seemed like it would go on forever. Then, as suddenly as it had started, it rumbled off into silence. There was not so much as a chicken cackle. Then—

"Judas Priest!" a voiced roared. "Alkali!"

Alkali scooped up his new binoculars. He prayed as he focused the glasses on the workshop entrance. Grampa had given him the binoculars for his tenth birthday. "Please God, don't let it be Grampa." The shop was filled with smoke. Particles of soot and dust drifted lazily out the shop door. A large, dark form dismounted the little garden tractor: slow, deliberate, ghostlike. Dad or Grampa? The distant slamming of screen doors made him turn his gaze in the direction of home. He saw his mother with his younger brother, Timmy, hurrying toward the workshop. He panned with the binoculars to his grandparents' house and caught Gramma on her way over to investigate the commotion. He watched her scurry as she wiped her hands in the folds of her apron. All the arrivals stopped at the workshop entrance. They just stood there looking inside and blocking his view. Then everything went dark.

Alkali dropped the binoculars and stared directly at a pair of blue denim legs. Dad stood towering in front of the cave entrance.

"I believe your grandfather is calling," he said.

Alkali could not count the times his dad had reminded him about "showing some judgement," and Alkali judged that at this particular time he was dead meat, anyway you sliced it.

"You heard me. Move it."

Slowly, Alkali crawled out of the cave with his binoculars swinging heavy from his neck. His dad made no move to help him up. It was not a good sign. Alkali followed his dad reluctantly to the workshop.

When they arrived at the entrance, Alkali could see that Grampa was in the midst of surveying the damage. The old Booker stove, which normally stood as solid as a rusted soldier, now lay in pieces on the floor. Sections of black metal stovepipe were scattered all over the cement floor behind the little, green tractor. It was easy to figure out what had happened. The black rubber tarpaulin straps were obvious evidence of the crime.

Alkali winced when he saw them wound around the legs of the old coal heater and hooked onto the tractor's mower attachment. It was also obvious that Grampa had not noticed this before putting the machine in DRIVE.

Everyone's eyes focused on Grampa's back. Dad turned and caught Gramma's eye, Gramma looked at Mom and Mom looked at Timmy. It was Timmy who broke the silence. He burst into fits of giggles. The others joined in. They could not stifle it. Alkali laughed as well.

Grampa spun around and glared. "What the blazes are you laughing at?" he bellowed.

Gramma stepped forward.

"James, you're solid soot from the top of your head to the seat of your pants," she said.

"Well, I'm glad you all find it so immensely funny," Grampa retorted.

The group quickly sobered.

"Come now. We'll have no words in anger," Gramma said calmly. "Let's go get you cleaned up." Gramma was the farm's resident diplomat. In his mind, Alkali whispered a word of thanks.

Grampa, ignoring her suggestion, reached for the closest pipe section. He picked it up and then stood looking somewhat bewildered. Where to start?

"Here. Give it to me," said Dad. "Alkali and I will clean up this mess."

Grampa looked at Gramma. She nodded her head in the direction of the house. Grampa shrugged his shoulders and snorted. He handed over the section of pipe. "And you," Grampa said, pointing his index finger at Alkali, "You make sure you *do* help your dad!"

Everyone stepped back in honor-guard formation to

allow Grampa's exit from the shop. Alkali fairly leaped to get out of the way and then stood watching his grandparents retreat, Gramma a few steps behind Grampa, who was still ranting and wildly waving his arms even when they finally disappeared into their house.

"I don't know how you do it, Alkali," sighed Mom. She held her hand out to Timmy to leave. Timmy looked up at Alkali with a satisfied smile on his face and said, "You going to get it now." Alkali knew he was already in too deep to punch him.

He turned and watched his dad realigning the stovepipe sections.

"I didn't do anything," said Alkali.

Dad glanced his way but continued at his task.

"I found the rubber straps with the hooks and I just wanted to see how far you could stretch them."

Dad just kept working.

Alkali stepped toward the mower and unhooked one of the straps.

"You're lucky he wasn't hurt," Dad said.

Alkali unwound the strap's rubber length from the coal heater's leg. He held it up like a dead snake.

"Boy, he sure was smoking," Alkali said.

Dad rose to his full height. He waved a section of elbow pipe in front of Alkali's nose. "Now look here. See the broken weld? When am I supposed to find time to fix it?"

Alkali quickly swung the rubber strap behind his back. He looked back at Dad with raised eyebrows. "I'll do it."

"Oh—right," Dad sighed. "Next thing I know you'll have burned the shop to the ground!"

Alkali looked over at the blackened blowtorch on the shop counter.

"Alkali," said Dad, "Don't get any ideas." He shook the pipe at him again. "And if this is all the help I'm going to get from you, the least you can do is go apologize to your grandfather. He's had a few minutes to cool off. Now, git!"

When Alkali was halfway over, he remembered the tarpaulin strap in his hand. Impulsively, he winged the strap toward the shelterbelt. It soared like a floppy boomerang, only it did not come back.

"There," said Alkali, satisfied he had seen the last of it.

CHAPTER
TWO

Alkali held the porch door open so it wouldn't slam and get Grampa even more riled. He stepped carefully over the sooty work clothes in a heap at the kitchen door.

"Now, I don't want you upsetting Helen over all this," he heard Gramma say. Alkali stopped dead. The voice was coming from the bathroom adjoining the kitchen. "She's having a rough go with this pregnancy, and she doesn't need more to worry about."

They were talking about Mom. Alkali waited to hear more, but someone turned on the bathtub taps. Carefully, he walked across the kitchen past the table toward the bathroom door. It was slightly ajar. Gramma was fussing with some towels. Grampa was already in the tub.

"You, of all people, to not check a machine over before starting it up," said Gramma.

"Oh, so now it's my fault," said Grampa.

Alkali stepped behind the door. He leaned forward just enough to see Grampa through the crack between the door and the jamb. Grampa looked silly, his face all blackened except for his white eyeballs. And below his neckline he was bare white, too.

13

"Alkali, the farmer's nuisance," he grumbled.

"And another thing," Gramma said, her voice growing louder as she moved toward the bathroom door, "that boy's getting too old for nicknames."

Alkali backed against the wall. He heard a cabinet door snap shut.

"His hair is just as white as ever," Grampa reminded.

"Alkali—" she said.

Alkali sucked in his breath.

Gramma walked across to the tub with some shampoo.

"What kind of a name is that for a young man? It was cute when he was little. But he's growing up. We should call him by his Christian name—James or Jamie," Gramma insisted.

Alkali edged toward the crack in the door. He was not going to miss this.

"There's enough confusion already with Jimmy and me," Grampa protested. "He can be James when I'm gone."

"Well, you can thank yourself for the confusion." Gramma's voice again grew louder. "You're the one who insists the firstborn sons be James."

Gramma stepped into the hallway, but the open bathroom door blocked Alkali from her view. He heard her footsteps ascend the staircase.

"Well," Grampa yelled after her, "Alkali will do just fine for now. The name suits him to a T." He chuckled to himself.

Alkali wished he had not heard Grampa. He watched the old man reach up and turn off the taps. He sat chest deep in a tub of grey scum. He squirted a golden glob of shampoo on the top of his normally shiny, bald head. Slowly, the glob was massaged into a crown of grey foam.

It reminded Alkali of old pictures he had seen in Gramma's photo album. Pictures of when Grampa had hair.

Grampa dipped his face into the murky water and surfaced without the blackened skin, without the black in his bushy eyebrows, without the soot-caked lips. Lather ran down his neck and shoulders—the grey foam slithering like a snake toward the whiteness. Suddenly, he rose from the water, leaving behind islands of bobbing foam. Alkali stood mesmerized by his grampa's nakedness. Except for his head, neck and forearms, his body seemed pearlescent. It reminded Alkali of a seashell Gramma had brought back for him from Hawaii. She had explained how it had once contained a living creature.

Grampa lightly rubbed his belly. He grimaced.

"Effie," he bellowed. "Bring the Maalox, would you? My stomach's acting up!"

He drew the shower curtain across. The plumbing groaned in protest as he opened the drain to release his bath and at the same time turned on the shower.

Gramma came clomping down the stairs and turned toward the bathroom. She was carrying a huge pair of boxer shorts. This time she saw Alkali standing there.

"Coming, James," she said. She looked directly at Alkali.

Alkali swallowed. "I just come to—"

Gramma lifted her finger to her lips. "Shh." Then she waved her hands at him to leave.

Alkali turned obediently and left. If she didn't want him to apologize, it was fine with him. But he felt crummy. Hearing what he'd heard. Seeing Grampa naked. White. And those enormous boxer shorts.

CHAPTER
THREE

Alkali woke to the sound of a spoon tinkling in a coffee cup. He heard Grampa and his dad talking.

"That boy is going to lead me to an early grave, Jimmy," he said.

"You can't die young, Dad, you always tell us you're going to live to be a hundred," said Jimmy.

"Right you are. And don't you forget it."

"I didn't. You did," Jimmy reminded him.

The low rumble of their laughter was familiar. Grampa always rose early, had his customary breakfast of corn flakes at his house and then arrived promptly at ten after seven every morning to have coffee with Jimmy. Together the two men would plan the day and compare notes on the local gossip.

Alkali sat on the edge of his bed and practiced saying sorry.

"I'm sorry, Grampa." No—too soft.

"I'm sorry, Grampa!" No—sounded like he didn't mean it.

"Grampa, I didn't mean for anything to happen." There—that was good.

Rubbing the sleep from his eyes, Alkali made his way to the kitchen, his white-blond hair sticking out at all angles, body bare except for drooping blue gotch. Numerous pairs of pajamas lay in his chest of drawers. On rare occasions, like visits to his city grandparents, he would concede and wear PJ bottoms, but usually it was just gotch. That's all his dad wore and that's all his grampa wore and that's all he needed. Mother did not approve.

Seeing his dad and grampa sitting at the kitchen table, Alkali stopped at the doorway to think about how similar the two men were. Both in denim work clothes— one was just an older and balder version of the other. He wondered if he would be like them.

The two men looked up at Alkali.

"Grampa—" Alkali started.

"Good morning, Alkali!" Grampa responded.

"Grampa—"

"Alkali. Apologize to your grandfather," Dad interjected.

"I'm trying," Alkali protested.

"Don't be cheeky." Dad got up and walked over to where Alkali was standing. "Tell your grampa you're sorry." He placed his hand on the boy's shoulder. Alkali felt dwarfed by his father.

"Oh, Jimmy, come on now. I really should have checked the tractor over before I started it up," said Grampa.

"Grampa—I didn't mean for anything to happen." Alkali finally got it out.

"You're just lucky I'm indestructible." Grampa stuck out his chest and beat it with a clenched fist. Then he patted the front pocket of his dark blue work shirt and reached inside. "Here's a stick of gum."

"Thanks, Grampa." Alkali was pleasantly surprised with how well things were going.

"Now, Alkali, I want you to come sit beside me."

Alkali obediently did as Grampa requested.

Grampa cleared his throat and stared into the boy's eyes. "I've got some bad news."

"What do you mean Grampa?" Alkali was confused.

"Your cat Blacky is dead.

Alkali felt sick.

"She's gone, son. I found her on the yard approach with a dead gopher in her mouth. She must have been hit by a car or truck."

Blacky was his favorite. The rest were all barn cats, wild strays. Alkali had gotten Blacky from the MacDonald twins up the road. He had got to hold her and feed her and pet her since she was a kitten. Blacky was his and now she was dead. He couldn't believe it. He felt sick to his stomach.

Dad leaned across the table and gave Alkali's hand a gentle squeeze.

"I'm sorry about your cat, Alkali. I know how much she meant to you."

Alkali's eyes started to blur. Quickly, he rose from the chair and headed for his bedroom. He threw himself on the unmade bed and cried.

When he could cry no more, he lay there and thought about how awful he felt. Not just that his eyes stung and his head ached, it was a deeper feeling—in his chest. This feeling was worse than last summer when Blacky's first batch of kittens hadn't made it. One kitten died when it was born, one disappeared (Dad thought an old tomcat must have killed it) and the last died of distemper. The distemper had been awful. The kitten's eyes got all yucky and crusted, then it got a cough and got real weak and died. All these things were awful, but they did not compare with the ache he felt now. Then suddenly it dawned on him—Blacky's second batch of kittens. Where were they? Who was going to look after them now? Alkali hit himself on the forehead with the palm of his hand. How stupid could he be to forget about Blacky's babies!

Quickly, he slid off the bed and threw on yesterday's clothes. He knew exactly what had to be done. First, he had to find Blacky and give her a proper funeral and then he had to find her kittens.

Her second litter had been born just two weeks ago. She must have been preoccupied with returning to her kittens after she caught that gopher. Alkali wondered if someone hadn't deliberately tried to run over her. Blacky was a smart cat, and it was difficult to accept that she could have gotten herself killed.

Returning to the kitchen, Alkali found his dad poring over the used implement section of the *Western Producer* newspaper. Grampa had already left to do his chores. Mother stood by the sink rinsing off the breakfast dishes. He could see Timmy in front of the television in the family room, engrossed in the early morning cartoons.

"Dad, could you help me give Blacky a proper burial?" Alkali asked. "We could dig a hole out behind the Quonset where Timmy's puppy is buried."

Mother turned from her task. "Alkali, you look terrible."

"Can we, Dad? Please," Alkali begged.

Dad nodded his head, got up and the two headed for the door. Just then Timmy raced into the kitchen.

"Can I go, too?" he asked.

"No! She was my cat." Alkali continued on his way out the door.

"I let you watch when we buried Dixie," Timmy persisted.

"That was different. I cared more than you did." Alkali slammed the door.

Timmy yelled, "You did not!"

Dad and Alkali searched the road and the approach where Grampa said he had found Blacky. No Blacky. They searched the ditch on either side but found nothing. It seemed odd.

"You don't suppose a coyote or an owl could have picked her up?" said Alkali.

"Not this fast," said Dad.

Together they walked back into the yard. Alkali glanced around, still looking. That's when he noticed the smoke coming from the rusted garbage barrels. He stopped. His father put his hand on his shoulder and Alkali knew instantly what had happened to Blacky. At first he felt shock, and then the tears came once again. He pulled away from his father's touch. Sobbing, he ran for the comfort of his cave.

It was sometime before he reappeared in the kitchen. He slumped in a chair.

Mom left her pot simmering on the stove and sat beside Alkali.

"Dad told me what happened, Alkali," she said.

"Why'd he do it?" said Alkali.

"Grampa feels differently about animals. He's lived a long time and, living on a farm all his life, he's a practical man. If Grampa loved every calf, every chicken—how could he part with them when it came time to sell?" she explained.

"Cows and chickens are different. They're dumb," Alkali argued.

Mom sighed. "Why don't you talk to Grampa. Maybe he'd best speak for himself."

Alkali was shifting out of sorrow; he was slowly slipping into gear for anger. *Talk to him. Talk to him. Better than that,* he thought to himself, *I'll show him!*

Out the door and to the garden he ran. Arriving there he hesitated. No sign of Grampa. He surveyed the carefully laid out plot. The dark green corn stalks stood tall on the far side; beside these Grampa had his potato plants in absolutely perfect rows. The beans, the carrots, the peas, all the same, perfect. Alkali's eyes set on the tomatoes. Grampa always grew the biggest, reddest tomatoes and everyone knew it. Just last week he had bragged that first prize at the horticultural fair was in the bag.

Grabbing a hoe, Alkali flew at the tomatoes. He hacked and slashed; he chopped and squished. Stakes and leaves were crushed in his rampage. The damage was complete in no time.

"ALKALI!"

Alkali sucked in his breath and wheeled around. Grampa stood not four feet away. Alkali looked back at the tomatoes, what remained of them. He saw the hoe in his hands. He dropped it. Then he threw himself at Grampa and pummeled him wildly.

Grampa wrapped his arms around the thrashing body.

"Whoa boy! Whoa!" Grampa, strong as he was, moved in the pattern of wild anger, tilting forward and back. Then, off balance, down they fell, the two of them, into the ruined tomato patch. Grampa held tight, his grip firm as ever. Alkali started to lose strength. The thrashing turned to rolling back and forth, then to gentle rocking. Finally, it was over. The two bodies heaved with labored breathing. Grampa held tight.

Grampa panted, "You okay?"

"You," Alkali was choking on air, "you—can—let—go."

Grampa released his arms and lay back. Alkali, too, lay still beside him. Both closed their eyes as if to go back to sleep after waking from a nightmare.

"Oh, Grampa. . ."

Alkali turned to face him. Seeing the old man lying still beside him, lying in the destroyed foliage, Alkali was overwhelmed by the horror of it all. Putting his head on Grampa's heaving chest, he wept.

"I love you, Grampa."

Grampa jerked up his head. Then he gently placed his arm to cradle the boy's head and lay back.

CHAPTER
FOUR

Grampa and Alkali worked silently in the former tomato patch. Surrounded by the lush green of healthy plants, the now almost bare rectangular patch of brown earth was a vivid reminder of what had just happened.

Grampa broke the silence. "There, that about does it."

Alkali finished carrying his last load of broken plants to the compost heap and returned to help Grampa stack the still usable stakes by the garden shed. The broken stakes were hurled into the surrounding caragana hedge.

"Let's see if Gramma has those rhubarb pies out of the oven," Grampa suggested. "We've got some talking to do."

Halfway back to the house Alkali spoke. "Are you going to punish me?"

"Yes."

No more was said.

Gramma looked twice at the sight of her husband and grandson: black soil clung to their hands and faces; tomato juice and seeds and green grass stained their clothing.

"You fellas better clean up," she said. "Care for a fresh piece of pie, Alkali?"

Under normal circumstances nothing would have pleased Alkali more, but after this disaster and anticipating his talk with Grampa, all appetite was gone.

"No, thanks," he mumbled.

Grampa and Alkali headed for the bathroom to wash: Grampa first, then Alkali. On returning to the kitchen, they found the table set with two fresh pieces of pie, cut and served with a scoop of vanilla ice cream on the side. Gramma handed them each a dessert fork.

"Thanks, Effie. Could use a glass of milk, too, please," Grampa said. He made a face and gave his belly a quick pat.

Gramma raised an eyebrow. She got the milk and two glasses and set them in front of her two men. That done, she pulled up a chair to the table and sat. She was not going anywhere.

Alkali did not eat. Instead, he used his fork to draw lines on the ice cream. His face was expressionless.

"So, Alkali," Grampa began, "Talk!"

Alkali knew that the whole mess could have been avoided if he had just come to Grampa and talked in the first place. Now he was scared.

"It's because of Blacky," he started.

"I didn't kill your cat, son."

"I know that, Grampa. It's what you did after."

Grampa sat back in his chair.

Gramma, confused, asked, "What did you do to Blacky?"

Grampa said nothing.

Alkali stared at Grampa. "He burned her up, Gramma. Just tossed her into a garbage barrel and burned her up."

"Alkali, Grampa always does that with dead chickens or animals," said Gramma.

Alkali looked down at the melting ice cream. "Blacky was not just *any* animal, Gramma," he whispered, "She was mine."

Grampa spoke softly, "Alkali, when I found Blacky on the approach it was not a pretty sight. It was even hard for me to tell it was Blacky. I didn't want you to see her like that. I couldn't leave her there for you to find."

As Grampa continued his explanation, Gramma got up from the table. Alkali watched her rummage in the drawer where she kept her papers.

"Once Blacky was dead, it didn't matter to her what happened. She's in cat heaven now," said Grampa.

Alkali thought about this, but to be tossed into a garbage barrel and burned still didn't sit right.

Gramma returned to the table, holding a handful of papers. As she spread them on the kitchen table, Alkali could see there was a whole bunch of words in little print covering every page. Down at the bottom there was hand-writing, Grampa's signature. Gramma's too. At the top of the page he could make out "University of Saskatchewan" in fancy letters.

Gramma sat down.

"Alkali," she began, "These papers mean that Grampa and I have decided that when we die we want our bodies to go to science."

Grampa chuckled, "You see, Alkali, this is the only way your old grampa could figure out a way to go to university."

"James!" Gramma scolded.

Alkali smiled weakly at his grinning grandfather.

"I want you to understand what I'm trying to tell you." Gramma sounded serious.

Alkali nodded.

"Grampa and I believe that when we die our souls will go to be with God. What happens to our bodies, the shell, doesn't really matter. But we feel if our bodies can be of some use, they should be used. At the university they'll use our bodies to help students learn to become doctors, doctors who can help others live healthy lives. When the university is finished with us, our bodies, they will cremate our bodies—that means burn them—and we have asked that our ashes be spread here, back home on the land. That is our wish. So you see, Grampa didn't feel any different about your cat, or your cat's body, than he does his own body. Do you understand, dear?"

Alkali looked down at the melted mess on his plate. Pushing away from the table, he felt guilty for not eating Gramma's offering. But he felt a bit calmer, a bit grownup.

"I have to go do some thinking," he said.

"That's okay, dear," said Gramma. "Come back later if you like."

Alkali walked over to his grandmother. Placing his arms around her shoulders and placing his cheek against hers, he gave her a hug. Skipping over to Grampa, he did the same thing and then headed to the porch.

Gramma turned to Grampa. She reached across and attempted to brush the dust and a piece of straw off his collar.

"Were you two fighting?" she asked.

Alkali did not want to hear Grampa's answer. The wooden screen door slammed as he left.

CHAPTER
FIVE

Alkali headed off in the direction of his cave. His eyes automatically scanned the ground, always on the lookout for potential treasures even though his mind was more on what Gramma had just told him.

"Did ya find the kittens?" Timmy yelled from the back step of their house.

Alkali stopped in his tracks. He had forgotten.

"Go ask Mom if you can help me look for them," he said.

Timmy did not need to be asked twice. He was delighted. He leaped up and raced into the house. Most of the time Alkali treated Timmy like an unpleasant chore. Especially lately; he was constantly getting Timmy dumped on him. Since the school year had ended, the standard line was: "Your mother is having a difficult time with this pregnancy. You can do your part to help out." Not Alkali's idea of a summer vacation. The five-year spread between the boys placed a limitation on their playing together. Alkali pretty well had freedom to roam the farmyard, but Timmy's rule was to be within sight of the house. Sometimes, Mom trusted Alkali to watch

Timmy outside this limit, and today Timmy was in luck.

"She said okay!" Timmy yelled as he came out the door and bounded down the steps. He hopped around his big brother like an anxious grasshopper.

Alkali sighed.

Together, they went to the place Alkali had first discovered the kittens, Grampa's garden shed. Actually, it was Grampa who first discovered Blacky with her four new kittens under the shed. Alkali had taken them over to the house, but Mom had said, "NO CATS! Blacky can look after her own babies." So Alkali had dutifully returned them underneath the shed but only after he had examined and named each of them.

Fat Cat was the biggest of the litter, partly because she had longer, furrier hair. She was black with a little white face and four white paws. Scrappy was gray with glazed blue eyes, and he seemed to be pushy, aggressive. He mewed the loudest, too, as if to say, "Hey, look at me!" Then there were the twins—at least they looked like twins, exactly the same, completely black all over. They were also smaller than Fat Cat and Scrappy. Timmy had called them Sweets and Mickey, two names that made no sense at all to Alkali, but Timmy seemed to be able to tell the two apart. You had to respect that. Alkali already had Blacky for his own, so he figured, to be fair, he'd let Timmy have the twins. Timmy had been thrilled.

Alkali returned the little family under the shed, but Blacky, with a new mother's protective instincts, had moved her kittens immediately and Alkali and Timmy had never found her new hiding spot. The adults had reassured them that the kittens would eventually surface when Blacky was ready. That was over a week ago.

Timmy and Alkali lay on the dirt, peering under the shed.

"They're not here," Timmy whined.

"I can see that, stupid!" Alkali snapped. "Let's check the barn."

As they were leaving the garden, Timmy noticed the bare patch in the garden.

"Where's Grampa's tomatoes?" he asked.

Alkali did not answer.

The two boys searched for the rest of the afternoon—the barn, the Quonset, around and underneath the granaries, by the gas tanks, the shelterbelt. After supper they continued the search but no luck. As the sun dropped on the horizon, Alkali made the decision to ask Grampa.

He had avoided going to him because of the episode earlier in the day. The matter of punishment had not been dealt with, and Alkali really didn't want to provide the opportunity for it to come up. But then, maybe Grampa knew the kittens' whereabouts.

Alkali headed over to Grampa's and was about to knock on the frame of the screen door when Grampa drove up in his truck. Hoping that Grampa's memory was short on tomatoes and long on kittens, he approached the old blue pickup and leaned in the open window.

"Grampa, have you seen Blacky's kittens?"

"No, I haven't, Alkali."

Just then Timmy caught up with Alkali and hopped onto the truck's running boards.

"Hello, Timmy," said Grampa.

"I can't find them anywhere. Me and Tim—"

"Timmy and I," Grampa corrected.

"Timmy and I," Alkali repeated, "have looked over

and under the whole farm. They'll die if we don't find them. Won't they, Grampa?"

The two boys stared at Grampa with worried eyes.

"They'll show up," he reassured them. "When they get hungry, they'll come out. They should be old enough."

"You think so?" Alkali, not truly satisfied, turned to continue his search. He knew the kittens could not survive without their mother.

"Alkali," said Grampa.

Alkali stopped and turned to face his grandfather.

"I've been thinking about my tomatoes," said Grampa. "This will be the first time in over fifteen years that I won't take my prize tomatoes to the fair. You're worse than a hailstorm, boy.

"I think that a suitable punishment would be to put you to work. I've talked it over with your dad and he's in agreement. You are going to clean my chicken coop. I don't care how long it takes, I want it done and I want it done right. It will have to pass my inspection. You'll start tomorrow morning. Understood?"

Alkali kicked at the ground. "Understood, Grampa."

Timmy stood with his mouth open.

Then Mom called and Alkali was glad to have a reason to leave. The search would have to end anyway because it was getting dark. Now he had even more on his mind. He walked toward home, wondering what awaited him there.

The chicken coop—how long would that take? Usually Grampa and Dad did it together. But it was Timmy trailing behind who really echoed his biggest concern.

"When are we going to find the kittens?"

CHAPTER
SIX

The next morning was a perfect day. Alkali stared out his bedroom window at the clean blue sky. He thought about asking Mom to go to Nickle Lake Park. Maybe they could even call the MacDonalds to join them. They could swim and have a picnic. Then he remembered—he had to clean the chicken coop. He rolled over in bed, his face in the pillow. He could just picture it. When school started at the end of August and he got the usual "What I Did On My Summer Vacation" assignment, he'd be able to write about spending his entire summer in the chicken coop. He stalled in his bedroom as long as he could stand it. Time to move out. Plodding to the kitchen, he thought about last night. His parents had not said a word about his fight with Grampa. He wondered if that was what was waiting at the kitchen table: a free lecture.

Grampa and Dad sat at the kitchen table as always. They were waiting for him.

"Best get some breakfast into you and get dressed," greeted Grampa. "I'll go get my truck." Grampa gave a mischievous wink at Jimmy and got up to leave. "You bring the wheelbarrow from the shop. I'll meet you at the coop and show you what has to be done."

"Wear your work clothes, Alkali," Dad reminded, "*Old* work clothes." He pushed the box of Shreddies toward Alkali's spot at the table. Alkali poured out a healthy helping, added some milk and sprinkled on as much brown sugar as he thought he could get away with. He felt a great sense of relief as he took the first spoonful. He had been spared the speech on responsibility.

The old wooden wheelbarrow was heavy and awkward, but he managed to get across the yard. Alkali really had to steer because the slightly flat rubber tire seemed to have a different idea of where it was going. The spade he brought along fell out several times. By the time he reached the coop, he was already sweating. The sun was shining brightly, and it was a rare day on the prairies, not a wisp of wind. It was a perfect day for the beach.

Grampa's old blue truck was parked in front. The tail-gate was down and opened out to the coop door. Grampa sat waiting on the open tailgate, his eyes closed and his face upturned to absorb the sun's warmth. His quiet moment was interrupted by Alkali's arrival.

"You use a spade to dig dirt, Alkali. Besides, the handle's too long. Use this." Grampa reached into the truck box and pulled out a well-worn shovel. "Here."

The chickens strained their necks in curiosity and murmured amongst themselves. Alkali felt like they were talking about him. "Stupid kid. Doesn't know the difference between a blunt-ended shovel and a pointed spade."

"Now, I don't want you to disturb my chickens," Grampa instructed. "All the straw on the floor and the chicken poop—shovel it into the truck box. I'll take it from there. We'll put in the fresh straw together." Grampa patted Alkali on the back and walked away.

Alkali stood momentarily outside the little red shack.

"I'll be back to check on you," Grampa called back over his shoulder.

Well, thought Alkali, *It sounds easy enough.* It was one task that he had never witnessed his dad and grandfather do, but he was confident that he would have no trouble. He peered in through the chicken wire door only to see twenty-six hens all simultaneously take one step backward as they peered intently back at him. "Dumb chickens," he whispered under his breath. Alkali lifted the hook latch on the door, and clutching the shovel, he stepped over the threshold into the dusty, dim shack. With this, the chickens flew into a frenzy.

Alkali watched the hysterical birds cackle and flap. One chicken in particular flew more than the others; it reminded Alkali of that expression "running around like a chicken with his head cut off." Alkali cocked his ear. Was that Grampa he heard chuckling off in the distance?

One thing he knew for sure, he could not work with twenty-six crazed chickens. He knew, too, that there would be lots of blood spots in the eggs this week if he couldn't get the dumb things to settle down. He looked around. Suspended particles of dust hung in the air—it was thick and choking. Alkali backed up to the entrance, hoping for clean air. The chickens, too, paused to regroup, but they never took their eyes off the intruder. Leaning at the entry, he pondered his predicament. He couldn't walk away: Grampa expected the job done. So he began to examine just what to do.

The far wall had three long horizontal poles where the chickens could roost. The chicken droppings that had collected below appeared about a foot deep. Along the right wall were the nesting hutches; he'd have to clean out the straw and junk. Yuck! The thought of sticking his hands in there. He was glad he had remembered gloves. It had never seemed so bad when he helped Grampa collect eggs. In fact, he had always thought of the chicken coop as a kind of fun place. But not today. The top half of the opposite wall was windows. The windows were so dirty— caked with straw, dust and bird droppings—that the glass was opaque. The light filtered down to a grey-brown oppressiveness except for a small opening that allowed in pure sunlight. This light played on the suspended particles of dust. A few chickens strutted out through the little doorway into the outdoor enclosure. They seemed to pause and fluff their feathers in indignation just before their exit.

"That's it!" Alkali exclaimed in delight. A few chickens squawked in alarm, reminding him to settle down. Alkali plotted in silence. *I just have to herd them all out into the outside pen and then block off the doorway,* he thought.

Alkali looked around for a suitable object to barricade the small opening. His eyes focused on the chicken's water pail. That would do the trick. Just in time—several chickens were eyeing his shoelaces as potential lunch. So Alkali set to work shooing chickens out of the coop. The chickens were not at all cooperative and the job was exasperating. Their squawking protests were still ringing in his ears when he finally shoveled his first scoop of manure. The smell of newly released ammonia was overpowering and just about knocked him flat. It made his eyes and nose run, but he kept on working. It was a treat to bring out the wheelbarrow loaded; the fresh outdoor air was like heaven. And so the morning continued, load after load.

By lunch time, the truck box was heaping with chicken manure and straw, but Alkali did not take time for a break.

"How's it going?" Grampa asked.

Alkali was startled by Grampa's voice. "Fine," he answered. He turned to see Grampa peering in through the chicken wire door.

"See you figured out what to do with the chickens," Grampa remarked.

"Yep," said Alkali, as he continued shoveling.

"Looks like you're about half done," Grampa observed further.

"Yep," Alkali again replied. He lay the shovel down.

"Have you had lunch?" Grampa inquired.

"Nope!" Alkali brought out another load. Grampa stepped back to allow his passage.

"Lost your appetite?"

Alkali looked Grampa straight in the eye. "Right!"

It was only after Grampa had left and Alkali was heading back into the coop that he noticed the orange, insulated water jug left beside the entrance. Gratefully, Alkali drank the cold, reviving water, but he knew he dare not stop long. He was afraid he could not make himself go back into that sweatbox to finish the job he had started.

It was around four-thirty when Alkali finally finished up and removed the pail that barricaded the chickens in the pen. Cautiously, they returned one at a time. Their careful steps and stares made Alkali smile. As he turned to leave, he took one last look before latching the wire mesh door behind him. With the sun shining on the west side now, the coop appeared bright, even brilliant. He gazed with satisfaction. All the chicken manure was gone, fresh straw was in the hutches, the water pail and feed trough were scrubbed up shiny clean. The chickens even looked whiter! He had worked hard cleaning the windows, scrapping the crud and scrubbing till his fingers burned. Now the windows sparkled and the entire inside of the coop was bathed in glorious sunlight. He could never remember the windows being clean before. Grampa couldn't call him a nuisance now!

CHAPTER
SEVEN

Alkali could hardly lift his head off the pillow. His body ached all over. He looked at his clock radio. *Ten-thirty! That can't be right,* he thought, but the bright sunlight outside his window confirmed it. He had gone to bed immediately after a long shower and a quick supper and had slept like a dead man.

Now he was back in the land of the living. There was a weird but familiar smell. His curiosity got the best of him and he slowly rose from his bed.

Dragging his body down to the kitchen, he found the source of the smell. His mom was busy putting up pickles. The smell of dill, garlic and vinegar filled the air. It helped clear the smell of ammonia that he had thought would never leave his nose's memory. He looked at the counter cluttered with pickling jars and sealer rings. Several pails heaped to the brim with tiny cucumbers encircled his mother's feet as she worked at the kitchen sink. Timmy, sitting in the family room, was watching Mr. Dress-Up.

"Why didn't you wake me, Mom?"

Mother looked up and smiled. "Timmy tried. A little sore this morning?" she asked.

Alkali nodded his head and sat at the table. His Shreddies were waiting.

"Grampa's been looking for you. He's been in three times this morning wondering if you were up yet." Her attention turned to the stove. She picked up the jar tongs and checked over the steaming boiler pot. "He was complaining—"

"Oh, great," Alkali griped quietly, "Not good enough for him?"

"Quite the contrary, dear," she paused as she rearranged the pickling jars in the steaming bath so they weren't touching each other. "He was complaining that he might have to purchase twenty-six pairs of sunglasses. The chickens were squinting—everything's so bright!"

Mom and Alkali laughed at the thought of laying hens wearing sunglasses.

She put down the tongs and wiped her hands on her terry apron. "He even said you did a better job than your father did when he was your age and given the same punishment."

Alkali's mouth dropped.

"I know," said Mom, giving Alkali a little peck on the cheek. "I'm really proud of you."

"It was hard at first with those stupid chickens."

"I can imagine, dear. That's why the men always clean the coop in the evening once it gets dark. That's when the chickens roost up out of the way. So . . . apparently you outsmarted your old grampa."

Alkali grinned proudly.

Alkali caught Grampa as he drove into the yard in his pickup. He hopped onto the running board.

"You looking for me?" Alkali asked expectantly.

"What were you trying to do, sleep away the day?" Grampa teased. "Hop in, Alkali. The day's a wasting. I've got something to show you." Reaching across the seat, Grampa opened the door. It had been many summers since the outside handle had worked. Same for the window. Didn't bother Grampa. When it got too cold to drive with an open window, he parked the pickup in the Quonset for the winter. When spring arrived, out it came again.

Alkali jumped into the seat beside his grampa and slammed the heavy door shut. Grampa's big boot punched the gas pedal and the old pickup flew through the yard, heading toward the dugout at the north end of the farmyard, just beyond the shelterbelt. The dugout had been excavated about four summers previously.

Alkali had loved watching the huge machinery make the big hole in the ground. At first, when the earth movers scrapped away at the prairie, it seemed an impossible task. But by the end of the day, it was almost amusing to see the gigantic Euclid disappear into the depths only to see it appear on the other side with yet another load of earth. When it was all done, Alkali had asked his grampa if the dugout was big enough to bury his house in. Grampa had only replied, "Why?"

The big hole sat dry and empty until the following spring thaw. The melting runoff, the result of snow held by the shelterbelt, had filled the dugout that year and each year since. This had meant that Dad didn't have to haul water from town anymore. Dad had mentioned many times what a relief that was. But Alkali had always enjoyed riding shotgun for his dad and missed those trips to town in the big truck.

The other sad part about the dugout was that it was

out of bounds to kids—especially Alkali. Sometimes he got to go there with his dad though.

The first year the sides of the dugout had remained almost bare with the exception of the odd, determined weed. The following year more green surrounded the entire excavation; cattails poked through at the water's edge and ducks occasionally dropped in for a brief visit. Last year a muskrat had taken up residence, and Alkali had also seen other animal footprints frozen in the mud along the waterline.

Alkali was pleased to have the opportunity to visit the dugout—but why had Grampa chosen now? And the chicken coop—when was he going to mention it?

Grampa parked close to where his irrigation pump was set up. Alkali followed him down the bank, past the pipe. Then he heard the sound—soft little cries.

"You found the kittens!" Alkali yelled.

"Calm down, boy. Wait till you see where."

Grampa pointed to a clump of heavy growth. Alkali parted the swamp grass. There, in a large duck nest, lay four little kittens scrambling over each other.

"A nest, Grampa! Have you ever seen anything so silly? Cats in a nest? Blacky was really thinking when she moved them here."

The chorus of mews grew louder and more insistent. Alkali fell to his knees beside the nest of orphans.

"In all my years I've never heard or seen anything like it," said Grampa. "I came early this morning to start up the pump so I could irrigate my garden. I heard them, but I was just as surprised as you to see them."

"Oh, Grampa. It sounds like they're starving. We've got to feed them. Help me carry them to the truck."

Grampa did not move.

Alkali pleaded, "Please, Grampa. We have to help. They'll die if we don't, won't they?"

With a reluctant sigh, Grampa bent to pick up Sweets and Mickey. Fat Cat and Scrappy were already clawing the front of Alkali's shirt.

"Seems like a lot of trouble for some barn cats," Grampa grumbled.

CHAPTER
EIGHT

Gramma and Grampa were in the midst of an early lunch. This was their usual course of action when they intended to spend the afternoon in town.

The porch and inside door slammed at the same time. Alkali breezed into the kitchen oblivious to his disruption.

"Grampa, will you take me to town so I can take the kittens to the vet?" Alkali asked in earnest. "They're not eating!"

Grampa slowly set his fork and knife down beside his plate.

"Alkali, it's only been a day."

"I know, Grampa, but I can tell they're getting weak. Please, could you take me? Dad's got field work. Mom's not feeling good. You're not doing anything. Besides, you're going to town," Alkali persisted. "Please."

Gramma gave Grampa a look as if to say, "I think you should."

Grampa gave a look as if to say, "No damn way."

Gramma returned an impatient look. "Do it."

Grampa sighed in resignation and then nodded his head to Alkali.

"Thanks, Gramma!" said Alkali.

"Now, why are you thanking her?" Grampa complained.

The trip to town was uneventful. Grampa drove the truck his usual ten kilometers per hour slower than the posted speed limit. Alkali sat quietly in the middle, hovering over his box of kittens. They were much quieter than on their last ride, and this left him even more worried.

Grampa and Gramma admired the maturing crops.

"Look at that Durum." Grampa pointed to his field by Nickle Lake, "She's really starting to fill out now. Another shot of rain would give us a forty bushel crop."

"Yes, let's keep our fingers crossed," Gramma answered as she thought of new drapes for her living room.

It was that time of the year for optimism. The weather had been kind so far, and the predicted grasshopper infestation had not appeared in their area.

When they arrived in town, Gramma was dropped off at the drugstore to get prescriptions refilled. Then she was to pick up the mail. They decided to meet at McBride's Grocery.

"Good—it's not busy," Grampa sounded relieved as they pulled up in front of the animal clinic. He held the door for Alkali as he carried in his precious cargo.

"Hello, gentlemen!" a pleasant-looking young woman greeted them as she came around the counter to look in the box. "What have we here?"

"Orphans, Dr. Thomson," Alkali said. "Their mother's dead, and I can't get them to eat. I'm afraid they'll die."

"Humph," Grampa snorted, "I don't think it's as bad as all that."

"Well, maybe we'd best take a look at them and see," said Dr. Thomson. "Let's go to the examination room."

The vet led the way into a side room. Alkali followed with his box, and Grampa reluctantly went along with them.

Carefully, Alkali lifted the little balls of fluff onto the Arborite-covered table. Dr. Thomson turned on the large overhead light and focused it on the brood. The kittens appeared to be shivering even though it was not cold. Alkali thought they must be scared. One by one she picked up the kittens and checked them over thoroughly.

"How long have they been without their mother?" Dr. Thomson asked.

"Four days," Alkali said gravely.

"They look pretty good, considering," Dr. Thomson reassured him. She held Mickey to her chest and stroked his fur.

"I'm going to de-worm them now." She proceeded to drop a tiny white tablet down Mickey's throat. She did the same thing to the rest.

Alkali watched over these proceedings like an anxious parent. He was amazed at her skill in getting each kitten to open its mouth.

"How do you do that? I can't get them to eat," he lamented.

"I suppose you've just set a dish in front of them and tried to get them to drink on their own," she suggested.

Alkali nodded his head. Sometimes he had felt more like he was drowning them in the saucer. They'd come up with their whiskers covered with milk and they didn't even attempt to lick their faces clean like Blacky would have.

"They're used to their mother nursing them. They're too young to drink on their own. They still have to suck. You're going to have to feed them with an eyedropper until they're a little older and can feed themselves." Turning to Grampa, she said, "Mr. Johnston, I suggest we try this feline formula. Cow's milk is too hard on their digestive system at this point." She picked a white jar off the display counter.

Grampa reached for the jar. "How much will this set me back?"

"It's fifteen dollars, sir." Dr. Thomson started to fill out charts on her patients.

"Fifteen dollars!" Grampa exclaimed.

"Yes, sir, but it should last until the kittens are ready for cat food mixed with cow's milk. This is dry formula you mix with water. The directions are on the jar," Dr. Thomson explained.

Alkali looked at Grampa with a pleading look.

"How do you propose to pay for this, boy?" Grampa asked.

Dr. Thomson busied herself with the charts. The kittens sniffed and mewed on the counter, not realizing their fate hung in the balance.

"I could do chores for you, Grampa. I'd do anything. Maybe the chicken coop will need cleaning again soon," Alkali answered.

"I suppose it will," sighed Grampa. "Okay, we'll take it." Grampa dug into his back pocket for his wallet.

Alkali happily gathered up his brood.

"One more thing, Mr. Johnston," Dr. Thomson cleared her throat, "These kittens are very young. At this stage their mother would be keeping them clean. Normally, the

licking of their anal region would stimulate their first—"
"Forget it!" Grampa interrupted abruptly.
Dr. Thomson smiled. Alkali snickered.
The bill was paid and gathering what little dignity Grampa could muster, they departed for McBrides, Grampa muttering, the kittens mewing.

CHAPTER
NINE

Grampa strolled into the workshop and did not seem too surprised to find Alkali kneeling on the cement floor.

"He's turning this place into a kitty nursery," Grampa yelled to Jimmy, who was just a pair of feet sticking out from under the combine parked in front of the shop door. Jimmy grunted. It suited the men just fine. This way they could work on the machinery in peace. Usually, Alkali was hanging over their shoulders asking questions until they could take no more: "How does this work? What does that do?" Now he was preoccupied with his mission of mercy.

"How are they today?" Grampa asked.

"Well, they're eating real good," said Alkali. "Look at them; they wear as much as they drink!" Alkali reached over into a dish of water where he was soaking some paper toweling. Carefully, he picked up a wet square and rung out the excess water. "They don't like the dropper," he said. Then he picked up one of the frolicking balls of fur. Gently he began to wash the squirming kitten, starting with the face and whiskers. He finished up with wip-

ing its little bottom. At this point Alkali screwed up his
nose in distaste.

"Meow," protested the little kitten.

"Sorry, Mickey."

The task done, Alkali placed the reluctant patient
into the little box he had fixed up as a crib.

"You'll make a wonderful mother," Grampa joked and
made his way over to the workbench.

Before continuing with the next kitten, Alkali stopped.

"Grampa, I'm kind of worried. The newspapers are
usually wet, but I've never cleaned up any—you know—
poop!"

Grampa looked up from the vise where he was trying
to straighten a steel blade. "Be grateful," he chuckled.

"It's not funny," Alkali said. "I've done everything Dr.
Thomson told me, too." He sat quietly and watched his
babies.

Grampa unscrewed the piece of steel and held it up to
the light sideways. He examined its length.

"Would you take us into the vet? Today?"

Grampa turned and looked impatiently at the boy.

"Your dad and I are fixing the combine, Alkali. I can't
just drop everything to suit you."

"No, I suppose not," Alkali whispered.

Grampa started for the doorway. He paused and
looked out at the combine, then back at the boy and the
kittens. Last, he gazed out at the sky.

"Okay. If it rains," he sounded irritated. "I can always
pick up the parts we need at the same time. Finish what
you're doing and be ready if it does rain."

Alkali looked doubtful. He could see through the
shop windows that there wasn't a cloud in sight.

Rain came exactly three hours later. It wasn't a great downpour, just enough to settle the dust and give the crops some relief from the hot sun. But Grampa showed up with his old blue pickup just as he had promised.

Alkali could not believe his luck as he shoved the box of kittens across the seat and jumped in behind.

"How did you know it would rain Grampa?" Alkali asked.

"My knee," Grampa said. "I get a twinge when the weather changes, even with my medicine."

"Hey, that's kinda neat," said Alkali. "It would be great to be able to predict the weather."

"Oh, sure," Grampa snorted, "It's just wonderful."

Alkali did not attempt any more small talk. He sat back in his seat and enjoyed the ride. The land was green-gold and alive. A half-formed rainbow hung in the sky. The air rushing in the open window was so easy to breathe. His kittens, secure in their box, were lulled to sleep by the easy motion of the truck. Alkali felt it couldn't get better.

Grampa drove directly to the vet's. As they wheeled in and parked beside the building, he groaned.

"Oh, great!" he moaned, "Look who's here—Walt Begley."

"What's wrong, Grampa?" Alkali asked. Mr. Begley was one of his grandfather's good friends.

"Nothing. Nothing at all."

Once again Grampa held the door while Alkali carried in the box.

"Well hello, James," boomed Mr. Begley as they entered the waiting room. "Didn't expect to see you here today! And how's Alkali? What you got there, boy?"

Immediately, he was over investigating what was in the box.

"Good day, Walt," Grampa replied, steering Alkali away and toward the examination room. "Dr. Thomson," he said.

The vet was behind the counter, looking up something in a glossy supply catalogue. "What can I do for you today, Mr. Johnston?"

Alkali held up the box.

Grampa lowered his voice. "Could you take a look at these critters? Right away? I'm kind of in a hurry." Then a bit louder he said to Walt, "You don't mind if Alkali goes ahead, do you, Walt? I've still got parts to pick up."

"Why, no," Walt replied, off guard, "I'm just in to order some chemical for those dang flies. They're driving my cows crazy."

Alkali felt his grampa propel him into the side room.

"You don't say," Grampa said as he moved out of the way for the vet to pass.

Alkali watched his grampa close the door behind her.

"Have you tried that new stuff?" he heard Grampa ask.

Alkali knew that his grampa and Walt would have no trouble passing the time waiting. Before he even got the kittens out of the box and onto the examination table, he could hear them discussing the merits of some new chemical. Soon, they'd be through with cows and onto crops and combines and the price of grain. The same stuff they talked about whenever they chanced to meet.

"What seems to be the problem?" Dr. Thomson asked as she held up Fat Cat. "I think they're looking wonderful. You've done a good job, Alkali."

Alkali turned his attention to the doctor. He was

pleased with her assessment and a little embarrassed to admit now that he wasn't doing as good a job as she thought.

"Umm," Alkali hesitated.

The vet looked at him expectantly.

"They're a—they haven't—a—" Alkali stammered, "pooped yet." There, he'd said it.

"Oh," she said. She moved her fingers over Fat Cat's body and palpitated his tummy. Last, she examined the kitten's bottom. "I think the problem can be easily rectified."

Alkali felt relieved. He had been afraid that maybe she'd have to operate or something.

Dr. Thomson set her patient down and went to a cupboard. She got down a small plastic bottle. It had a long green nozzle on the end. Next she went to the sink and started to run some water. She seemed to be testing its temperature with her wrist.

The kittens busily sniffed the examination table and peered over the edge. Alkali watched them as he eavesdropped on Grampa and Walt. Actually, you couldn't help but hear them. He thought about how loudly old men talked. He began to wonder why Grampa had acted so weird. Shoving him into the room like he didn't want Walt to see the kittens. Strange.

Dr. Thomson returned with the bottle filled with tap water. She reached for Scrappy and held him down on the table firmly with one hand. With her thumb and fingers, she lifted his tail and quickly inserted the nozzle of the plastic bottle into the kitten's bum.

"Yeoow," the kitten protested.

Alkali was stunned. Nothing had prepared him for

this. He watched her give the plastic bottle a gentle squeeze and then pull out the nozzle. It happened so quickly that he wondered if it had happened. Then he saw her do the same to Fat Cat.

"Meow!" Fat Cat knew for sure it was happening.

Next, Dr. Thomson reached for Mickey. "Alkali, you can put those two in the box now." She motioned her head in the direction of Scrappy and Fat Cat.

Alkali obeyed. By the time he had deposited them into their box, the other two had mewed in protest and were already up and sniffing about.

"There," said Dr. Thomson, "All done." She looked up at Alkali. "Don't look so worried. They'll be fine."

The kittens seemed to recover from the shock quicker than their master. He lifted Mickey and Sweets into the box and followed Dr. Thomson out to the waiting room.

Grampa was over like a shot.

"How much will it be, Doc?" he said, as if he were asking a secret. He pulled out the wallet from his back pocket.

"Twenty dollars covers it, Mr. Johnston," Dr. Thomson smiled as she started to write out a receipt.

"No need for that," he said nodding at the bill. He slipped a twenty onto the counter.

"Thank you, and you tell Alkali if he has any further problems, just bring the kittens in," she said.

"I don't think I can afford to tell him that," Grampa said dryly. "But thanks anyway."

Alkali was at the door. Mr. Begley got up and held it open for him. "Cute kittens, Alkali," he said.

Walt and Grampa exchanged goodbyes, and Grampa hurried out to the truck.

"So, tell me, Alkali, what did I just put out twenty dollars for?" He shifted into gear and pulled out of the clinic parking lot.

"I don't know, Grampa," said Alkali. He was looking at Scrappy; the kitten kept turning around and around. "Dr. Thomson took this bottle with a long tube sticking out of it, filled it with water and stuck it in the kitten's bums."

"An enema," Grampa started to laugh. "I paid twenty bucks for an enema!"

"Four enemas!" said Alkali, "And they didn't like it, Grampa." Alkali watched the kittens. Now Mickey was doing the same thing as Scrappy, round and round.

"No, I'll bet they didn't," said Grampa chuckling.

Soon, all the kittens were agitated, moving around in the box, up and over. Alkali gently pushed them back in with each attempt at escape. The kittens began mewing and grunting. Alkali glanced over at Grampa. Grampa looked back. Then they heard the sound of expelling fluid. Both Alkali and Grampa looked at the box in horror.

"Judas Priest!" Grampa muttered.

Alkali watched the box interior become a diarrhea disaster area: green-yellow slime was flying in every direction. The kittens mewed and clawed. The smell from the box was sweet and sickening, the kind of smell that makes you think about throwing up. Alkali turned to the open window, gasping for fresh air. He saw that Grampa was driving right by the John Deere dealership and was heading home.

"How do I let you talk me into these things?" he demanded.

The kittens were now frantically trying to scratch their way out. Alkali held his hands over the top of the box but the kittens were very persistent, their wet, slime green heads poking out here and there.

Just as Grampa turned on to the highway, there was a sudden downpour.

"Quick, Alkali!" Grampa barked. "Grab the cardboard from behind the seat and hold it over your window!"

Alkali did as he was told. He struggled to get the cardboard in place and still keep the kittens at bay. The windshield wipers worked overtime, trying to keep up to the rain. Grampa took an old rag and rubbed the glass.

"I really needed this, Lord," he said as he wiped and drove. No sooner had he finished than the windshield started to fog up again.

"Alkali, quit breathing!" he commanded.

Alkali, at that moment, would have gladly obliged if he could have. He sat quiet, his right side damp-cold from the downpour, his lap gradually becoming warm and wet as the yellow ooze soaked through the cardboard box.

When they pulled into the yard, Grampa parked in front of the workshop. He hopped out and held the door for Alkali.

Alkali carefully slid out of the truck, supporting the box underneath with both hands. The bottom was going to fall out at any moment. Once he was out, he looked back at the seat. He could see there was a big gold stain.

"I'm sorry, Grampa," Alkali said. "I'll clean it up right away."

Grampa shook his head. "You'd better look after those kittens first." He got back into his truck. "And you could use a bath yourself." He held his hands to his nose.

Alkali walked toward the shop to start his clean up job. He heard Grampa rev the engine and pull away. Then he remembered that he had forgotten to say thank you.

"Thank you!" Alkali yelled. It was too late. Grampa was already out of hearing range. *I'll catch him at the house*, Alkali thought.

He didn't dare take the box of kittens with him because it was ready to fall apart. He hurried into the shop and set them down. "Now you stay out of trouble until I get back," he warned, but the kittens were too busy mewing and scratching to listen.

Alkali ran out the door across the yard toward his grandparents' house. Grampa was already out of the truck and on the step at the screen door. Alkali stopped in his tracks. Gramma was inside the screen door. She wouldn't let Grampa in.

"Judas Priest, woman!"

Grampa was steamed.

When Alkali saw Grampa pull out his shirt from his pants and start to unbutton it, he knew for sure it was definitely not the time to drop in.

CHAPTER
TEN

The inside of the granary was starting to heat up. The brief coolness of the morning had evaporated into a cloudless, hot summer day. Alkali felt his shirt sticking to the sweat forming between his shoulder blades. His knees ached against the hard cement floor, but he just kept edging along the floor and the wall seam with the vacuum nozzle. He was too close to being finished to stop now. Grampa was sweeping the leftover kernels of grain into a pile and then scooping the gatherings into a feed pail with a metal dustpan. Later, he would mix in a bit of oyster shell and ground oats and feed the mixture to his chickens.

Grampa had recruited Alkali to help with preparations for the fast approaching harvest. Cleaning the big steel storage bins was number one on the list. At first Alkali was pleased; it was *men's* work. But the thrill was quickly wearing off. It was also *hard* work. Together, they worked in the dusty dimness, not talking. The noise of the vacuum cleaner echoing inside the steel walls discouraged all conversation and easily drowned out the humming of the portable electric generator located outside the granary. Grampa used hand signals to point out what he wanted done.

He tapped Alkali on the shoulder. It startled Alkali, who was concentrating on not missing that last stray kernel. Once he had Alkali's attention, Grampa pointed to the only exit—a small square door about two feet off the floor. Grampa picked up his pail and went to the doorway. First, he lifted the pail outside, then stiffly he lifted one leg over the metal threshold, stuck his head out and followed through, pulling the rest of his body into the daylight.

Alkali took a quick look around. The interior of the bin was cleaned to Grampa's specifications: "Not one single kernel of wheat left." He turned off the shop vacuum and pulled it over to the doorway. Grampa switched off the electric generator and leaned in to help lift out the vacuum.

"Looks clean," Grampa said as he hoisted the vacuum outside. Alkali followed through the opening easily.

"Why does it have to be so clean?" Alkali asked.

"Could end up with bugs or mould," Grampa said.

"Has it ever happened to you?" Alkali questioned.

"Yep." Grampa wound the electric cord around the vacuum.

"Which?"

"Rusty Grain Beetles!" Grampa looked up, exasperated.

"What did you do?" Alkali was fascinated.

"We had to put in poison pellets to kill them."

"How?" Alkali persisted.

"The Wheat Pool Centre gives you this special long pole to insert the pellets deep into the grain in the bin."

"Does it work?"

"Of course it works! Why else would we do it? And it costs money, too!" he exclaimed. "Judas Priest! Is that all you can do? Ask questions!"

"No, Grampa," Alkali sounded wounded. "I just want to know things."

"Well, the only thing I know for sure is those bins over there are waiting."

Alkali looked at the long row of giant, shiny granaries. It would take forever to get them all done. And Grampa—why was he so grumpy? *He should be glad I'm helping,* Alkali thought to himself.

Grampa motioned for him to help lift the shop vacuum into the back of the truck.

Their attention was diverted by an old maroon station wagon driving up beside them. Walt Begley got out from the driver's seat. Alkali could see Margaret Begley on the passenger's side. She appeared to be pinned to her seat by a huge floral arrangement of gladioli spears. She bent forward carefully so as not to disturb the blossoms and rolled down her window.

"Hello, James. Effie said we'd find you here!" Walt's voice boomed. "We're just on our way in to the fair. Not too late to change your mind. We'd be glad to take in your entries for you. Doesn't seem right, not to have the famous Johnston tomatoes to compete against!"

Alkali winced.

"Naw," said Grampa, "Thought I'd give Marg a chance at first prize this year."

"James Johnston!" Marg huffed, "That'll be the day! You just saw my garden this year and knew it wasn't worth your bother to even enter!"

They all laughed.

"What am I going to do with those two?" Marg asked Alkali. "By the way, how are your kittens? Walter said you had them at the clinic?"

"That's right. The trip home was a nightmare. The kittens started to leak all over the—"

"But they're just fine now," Grampa interrupted. "Isn't that right, Alkali?" Grampa stared hard at Alkali.

"That's right. They're . . ." Alkali looked puzzled. "They're just fine now."

"Good, I'm glad to hear it." Marg smiled. She looked down at her wristwatch. "My goodness, Walter. Look at the time."

Walter walked back to his side of the car. "Don't want to be disqualified for being late." He slid into his seat behind the steering wheel. "Alkali, don't let your grandfather work you too hard!"

"No," Alkali yelled back. "I like helping."

Marg quipped, "Well, comments like that should keep you in the will, dear." The adults laughed.

The station wagon roared as Walt turned on the ignition and with his foot still on the brake, floored the gas pedal. It sounded like it might blow up. Alkali and Grampa felt the blast of warm air gust from the car's exhaust.

Walt leaned across, peering through the floral arrangement. "Won't be the same without you, James!" he hollered over the engine's roar.

"Next year." Grampa hooted back. "Good luck. And thanks for stopping by!"

The maroon wagon lurched forward. Margaret Begley struggled to hold on to her vase. The couple waved as they left Grampa and Alkali in a small cloud of dust.

"Don't think Walter will ever learn how to treat a machine," Grampa muttered as he shook his head.

Alkali returned to lifting the vacuum onto the tailgate of the truck. He wanted to do it himself, but he didn't have enough strength for the last oomph. Grampa came over and gave it the extra boost required.

"It's my fault you're not going to the fair," said Alkali.

"Yes," Grampa snapped, "I guess I have you to thank, don't I?"

Alkali stared hard at the ground.

Grampa stood looking at Alkali. "No, there's other things I could enter boy. My heart's just not in it this year."

Alkali looked up at Grampa. There was a tiredness in his face he had never seen before.

CHAPTER
ELEVEN

The fields were dry and golden. The long stretch of hot weather had resulted in harvest arriving early, just as Grampa had predicted. This suited Alkali just fine because it meant he got to help; otherwise, he'd be in school and he'd miss the good stuff. And that wouldn't have been very fair after he had spent so much of his summer doing the boring stuff, like cleaning grain bins.

It was hard for Alkali to really choose what he liked best about harvest. Swathing the crop down was a dusty and buggy job because they didn't have a cab on the swather. He liked it the least, but even it was all right. Riding in the grain truck was fun, especially when they hauled to the elevator. Usually, Dad let him get a drink out of the pop machine in the grain buyer's office. But really, his two most favorite things were having meals in the field and riding in the new self-propelled combine with Grampa. Well, the combine wasn't exactly new; it had been through one harvest. It was huge and green— the ultimate in machinery. "Why, it costs as much as a house!" Gramma had said when the men first brought it into the yard. It was truly a marvel to watch when it rumbled into a field. The interior of the cab was deluxe. It had air conditioning, a huge upholstered seat with big comfortable armrests—that's where Alkali perched when he got to ride—a stereo radio, a citizens band radio and a whole console of buttons to push—like a computer. Alkali was still trying to learn what they were all for. Grampa insisted he'd never learn. It was a beautiful machine. Dad called it the Cadillac of combines!

Alkali sat swaying in the black, upholstered seat of the combine, turning the wheel, pretending and waiting. Waiting for Grampa. They were supposed to be out there harvesting. *What's taking him so long?* he wondered. Grampa had been all set to go to the field and then remembered he had forgotten his drinking jug. He seemed to be taking forever. Alkali saw him coming around the workshop with his jug, an old vinegar bottle Gramma had insulated by sewing a towel around it. Alkali did not understand why he couldn't use a thermos like everybody else.

"Alkali!" Grampa barked. "Get down here! Now!"

Alkali was bewildered.

"Now, Alkali!"

Alkali slid off the seat and out of the combine cab. Quickly, he descended the side stairs to where Grampa stood. He could see that Grampa was holding his jug in one hand and what looked like a strap in the other.

"Do you know anything about this?" Grampa demanded.

Alkali was afraid to say anything.

Grampa waved the black tarp strap in front of Alkali's face. "Well?"

"It's a strap, Grampa."

"I know that! I ought to use it on you!" Grampa's voice was getting louder. "Where do you think I found it?" Now he was yelling.

Alkali shook his head. *How do I know?* he was thinking, but he didn't dare say it.

"In the trees between here and the house."

Alkali instantly remembered the day he had winged the strap, and his face gave him away.

"I thought as much," Grampa said. "I knew it was you." Disgusted, Grampa threw the tarp strap toward the workshop entrance. It hit the siding and flopped to the ground just outside the doorway.

The lecture was interrupted by the rumbling arrival of the big grain truck.

Dad leaned out the truck window. "You guys plan on doing any work today?" he joked. "Let's go. Time's a wasting!"

"You go with your father," Grampa ordered.

Alkali made tracks over to the big truck.

"We'll go swath a few more rounds and give you a chance to get a load on!" Dad hollered to Grampa as he swung the truck toward the gate.

Alkali was glad to get away from the old man. Why'd he make such a big deal out of a tarp strap? Wasn't like it would kill anyone hanging there in the trees.

"Old bastard," Alkali mumbled just loud enough that Dad heard.

"Alkali!" Dad punched down the brake so hard that Alkali almost slid right onto the floor of the truck cab.

Alkali was in the process of regaining his seat when Dad reached across. For a moment Alkali thought his dad was going to slap him, but instead he opened Alkali's door.

"Out!" Dad shouted.

"He's always blaming me for everything," Alkali protested. "Nothing's ever—"

"Out now!" Dad repeated. "I don't have time for this! And you're lucky I don't! But get this mister: Don't you ever call your grandfather that again!"

Alkali, once again, found himself on the ground. *Twice in less than five minutes,* he thought to himself—*A new personal record.*

He headed for his cave. He did not watch his dad drive out of the yard nor did he look up as he walked past Grampa, who was now sitting high up in the combine cab.

Alkali was sitting in the cave when he heard the porch door at his grandparents' house slam several times. He saw Gramma going back and forth to the blue pickup truck.

"Lunch," Alkali said when he finally figured out what she was doing. He crawled out the entrance and ran to join her.

"Alkali," said Gramma, somewhat surprised as she came out carrying yet another cardboard box of goodies. "I thought you were with the men." She handed the box to him as he waited with his arms outstretched.

"Naw," he said, "I thought I might go out now."

"Well, I packed enough lunch for you." She turned and went back into the house. Alkali put the box into the back of the pickup. He saw the other boxes were loaded with plastic containers and sealer jars and cups.

Gramma appeared back on the steps.

"I guess that's it," she said, looking worried. It's been a year since I made lunch for the field. I keep thinking I've forgotten something." She walked around the truck and slid in behind the wheel. "Hop in, Alkali!"

Alkali hopped in, smiling as he anticipated the drive. She turned on the ignition and gripped the steering wheel with both hands. The old truck lurched and then stopped dead. She turned on the key again—this time flooring the gas pedal. She fiddled with the gear shift until it made a grinding noise and the truck jerked forward a bit, then a bit more and finally rolled ahead smoothly.

Alkali found it hard to relax as they rattled down the road. Gramma alternated her foot between the gas pedal and the brake. She would accelerate to forty kilometers per hour, then brake back to half the speed and then back to the gas pedal. He was glad it was a short distance to the field. If it had been all the way to town, it would have driven him crazy. Gramma did not talk when she drove. It was a quiet trip.

"There's the combine," Alkali pointed to the field off to the right. "Looks like they're just finishing up. They'll cross the road to the piece by the lake next. Park there."

Gramma took Alkali's advice. She parked alongside the outside row of swath.

Alkali wondered what Grampa and Dad would say when they saw him, but he was glad he came. Alkali loved this piece of land. The field ran along the shore of Nickle Lake. It was a beautiful sight. He had heard several people suggest to Grampa that he should sell the property for cottage development, but Grampa had said, "Over my dead body!" This always pleased Alkali because he secretly hoped that Grampa was saving it for him. Someday, Alkali would build his house there. Today, it was the perfect place for lunch.

Gramma immediately went to work setting out lunch

on the tailgate. She spread out a colorful tablecloth and lay out the feast she had prepared. Sealer jars filled with hot tea and thermoses of cold ice tea. Tupperware containers of sandwiches—roast beef, salmon, cheese—all made with thick slices of fresh home-baked bread. There were Gramma's special chocolate cupcakes. There was fruit: plums, bananas, nectarines.

The combine arrived shortly, bringing with it a whirl of dust. The big grain truck pulled in right behind.

"How's it going?" Gramma greeted Grampa and Dad.

"Good. Running good," Grampa said, walking toward them.

"I'd say at least thirty or thirty-five bushels to the acre," Dad added.

Alkali climbed into the back of the truck box as it provided him with the best access to the food. He perched on the wheel well.

"Help yourselves," Gramma said as she unscrewed the thermos top.

Alkali grabbed one of Gramma's cupcakes, quickly disposed of its paper wrap and shoved the entire chocolate handful into his mouth. His cheeks bulged out as he chomped.

"Ice tea, Alkali?" Gramma held out a cup and gave him a disapproving look. "You shouldn't try to eat it all at once."

"Mm orry Amma," Alkali said. He put one hand over his mouth to prevent cake crumbs from falling out and reached for the cup with his other hand.

"Alkali," Dad snapped, "you know better."

Alkali gulped down several times. "But I'm hungry!" he protested.

"You're not going to starve here. There's enough food to feed the Russian army," said Dad.

"Why are you feeding him anyway?" Grampa asked. "He hasn't done any work."

Gramma smiled. "Ignore him, Alkali. Have another one. I know you like them." She held out the Tupperware container. Eleven tiny, perfect chocolate cakes sat waiting to be eaten. Alkali eyed the cupcakes and reached out to pick up the one with the most icing.

"No more, Alkali," Grampa ordered. "You can wait until your dad and I have at least had one."

Alkali withdrew his hand and looked sheepishly at Gramma.

"Milk. No milk?" Grampa pawed around the jars and thermos bottles.

"I'm sorry, James," Gramma apologized. "I just knew there was something I forgot. I can go get some in a jiffy."

"Forget it," he snarled.

They were all surprised at the edge in his voice.

"Look, if you're not feeling well, go lie down for a bit," said Dad. "I can run the combine. Helen can drive the grain truck."

"I'm okay!" Grampa sounded more irritated. "Besides Helen doesn't need to be bouncing around a field in a grain truck in her condition. We want her to hold off on that baby until after harvest, remember."

"I can drive the grain truck!" Alkali piped up.

"Oh, that's a real comfort," Grampa snapped. "The thought of you behind the steering wheel."

"James," Gramma scolded.

"I know how to drive. You showed me," Alkali reminded him. "You even let me drive your truck.

Remember? When Dad was sick and we fed cows together."

"Alkali, all you did was steer and put your foot on the brake when I signalled. Besides, my truck and the grain truck are two different vehicles. Why, you can't even reach the brake and see over the dash at the same time on the big truck! You'd be an accident looking for a place to happen!"

Alkali looked down at the lunch. He knew his grandfather was right. He also knew it was against everything his grandfather had ever taught him to let a kid operate farm machinery. Grampa always said, "Accidents are caused by carelessness, but it's panic that kills." It angered him whenever he read in the paper about yet another farming accident.

"Alkali, driving the truck is the easy part," Dad said. "It's when you unload that the work starts—moving the auger, running the hydraulic. You're too young. It's too dangerous."

"The boy was just trying to help," Gramma said as she held out the container of fruit to him.

Grampa took a swig of his tea and then tossed what remained in his cup off into the stubble. He wiped his mouth with the back of his sleeve, reached for a couple of plums and stuffed them in his shirt pocket. He turned in the direction of the idling combine and walked toward it. He did not say another word.

Gramma, Dad and Alkali watched him make his way across the dusty stubble. All three were subdued by his silence.

Gramma saw the look on Alkali's face. "Grampa's not himself, Alkali."

"Yeah, I noticed," Alkali agreed.

Grampa did his usual walk around the big machine—disappearing out of their view.

Alkali reached for a cupcake. It seemed safe.

"Jimmy. I'm going to pack some lunch for your father," Gramma said as she gathered a sandwich and some fruit. "Maybe he'll want it later. He hardly ate a thing. And what little he did eat, he gulped down like it was his last meal."

"Fast eater, fast worker!" said Dad. "He'll never lose his hired man's habits."

"He eats too fast," said Gramma. I'm worried about him. I want him to go see the doctor, but you can't make him do anything. Especially during harvest." Gramma looked up toward the combine. "Now—where is he?"

They all looked up toward the combine.

"Maybe he's adjusting the belts," Dad suggested.

"Or taking a leak," Alkali said.

Gramma and Dad both gave Alkali an impatient look.

"Mom, if you're really worried, why don't you give Craig a call. See if he can arrange the time off. There's still a lot of acres to grind off. And Dad's right, I can't ask Helen."

"Well, your brother was certainly willing to come. Do you think I dare phone behind your father's back?"

Dad nodded his head. "Do it."

"There he is!" Alkali said as Grampa appeared from behind the combine. Grampa started to climb the combine steps. Halfway up he waved his arm in their direction and hollered, "Alkali! Are you coming?"

Alkali did not wait to be asked twice. "You bet!" he hooted. Scrambling off the tailgate, he leaped to the ground, carrying a sandwich in one hand and a nectarine in the other. He jogged over to the combine.

"Don't worry, Alkali, I'll leave extra lunch for you, too," Gramma called out after him.

Alkali waved back at Gramma and Dad. Grampa finished his climb up the outside ladder, slow and cautious. Alkali skittered up behind like a tree lizard.

The afternoon was gorgeous. Sun and blue sky. Blue sky as far as the eye could see. Alkali talked and ate. He was relieved that he was no longer in Grampa's bad books. Maybe it was just like Gramma said, maybe he just wasn't feeling well. But Grampa seemed all right now as he carefully drove the combine around the field, picking up the heavy swath.

"Good crop, huh Grampa! Should run forty bushels to the acre."

"Thirty-five at best, Alkali," Grampa corrected.

"It's still real good for second year stubble."

"You sound just like your father. He just got lucky. If we hadn't got that rain at just the right time, those fertilizer bills would be staring him in the face just as I predicted. The land can't take this continuous cropping. This is going to be summer fallow next year. I don't care what Jimmy thinks!" Grampa grumbled.

Alkali digested this pronouncement. He was learning to listen rather than offer any opinions that might differ with Grampa's ideas on farming. He'd let his dad hash this one out. Besides, it was Grampa's combine, and Alkali didn't want to jeopardize his opportunity to ride shotgun.

The combine swung around, and Nickel Lake came into full view.

"Look at the lake. Someone's water skiing!" Alkali pointed out.

"Would you rather be out there, boy?" Grampa asked.

"Nope," Alkali responded quickly, "I want to ride with you, Grampa."

"That's my hired man," Grampa patted Alkali's shoulder. "Call your Dad. Hopper's almost full. Time to unload," he ordered.

Alkali reached up for the CB radio. "Now this is more like it," he thought to himself. He turned down the squelch and held the mike to his mouth.

"52–30. Are you by? Calling 52–30. Are you by?"

"52–30. By." Dad's voice crackled over the speaker.

"Sod Buster, got a load for you."

"10–4, Alkali. On the way," Dad radioed back.

"Good job, Alkali," Grampa directed. "Here comes the truck. You swing out the auger for me."

Alkali slid off the armrest and pulled down on the black lever that protruded from the back of the seat. He watched the large pipe slowly swing out horizontally from the combine. Just then his dad drove up in the big grain truck. When the truck box and the auger mouth were lined up, Grampa pulled up on the yellow lever by his left foot. Out flowed the hard, golden kernels through the auger until the combine hopper was empty and the truck box was heaped high. Alkali found the smooth unison of the truck and combine very satisfying.

"52–29. I'm taking this load to the elevator. Want to come along, Alkali?"

"No, Sod Buster. I'll stay with The Boss," Alkali radioed back.

"That's a big 10–4! See you later!"

Alkali looked back out the side door window and waved to his dad. His dad gave a quick wave in return and then cranked the steering wheel of the big truck, driving it away from the combine's side. The three-ton truck lumbered under its load, heading in the direction of town, leaving its distinct trail of tire tracks and billowing dust.

"You should have gone with your father," said Grampa.

"Maybe next time."

"Sure," Grampa replied weakly. "But your Grampa's not feeling so good."

"I'll radio Gramma to bring you some milk." Alkali reached up for the CB mike. "I'll get Dad to pick up your Rolaids while he's in town."

"No!" Grampa barked. "Just leave it alone! I'll be fine. If you really want to help me, you could give that tongue of yours a rest. No more chatter—okay? My ear is starting to wear off!"

Instead of reaching for the CB mike, he turned off the CB power so the crackling static would not irritate his grandfather. They continued the round in silence. The only noise was the constant chugging of the combine as it ate up the swath.

Alkali sat back on the armrest and tried to act relaxed. It was hard not to fidget, and he now regretted his decision to not go with his dad. He tried to concentrate on the surroundings, hoping to catch a glimpse of a gopher or a rabbit scurrying by. He was distracted by Grampa's labored breathing. Grampa was staring straight ahead instead of watching below where the combine table lifted the swath off the ground. He was very pale, almost grayish white. The robust, tanned face looked drained. Tiny beads of perspiration trickled down his dusty forehead.

Reaching up to Grampa's forehead, but afraid to touch, Alkali whispered, "Are you okay?"

All of a sudden, volumes of bright red blood mixed with undigested food spewed from Grampa's mouth. The force of the retching was tremendous. Alkali drew his hand back in horror. The vomit ran down his arm. He looked at it, frozen like a statue. The floor, his boots, the front window, the instrument panel—all were covered with the red-orange vomit. The cab of the combine filled with a sickening stench. The feeling of nausea almost overcame Alkali.

Grampa made choking sounds, a snapping gurgle, then desperate gasps.

"Grampa!" Alkali yelled.

Grampa's body pitched forward against the steering wheel. Alkali grabbed at his shoulder and fought to lift him off the wheel. In his futile efforts to pull him back, his eyes suddenly caught sight through the splattered windshield of the direction the combine was drifting. Its wheels were following the lay of the land down toward the lake. The massive machine was chugging toward disaster. Alkali was seized with panic. If he didn't stop the combine, it would go over the edge and into the lake. The broken-down barbwire fence and the few prairie bushes that separated the field from the sharp drop-off were not enough to stop the combine.

Trapped in the cab, they'd drown.

He looked at Grampa and for a second wondered if he were already dead. Grampa's face was now contorted and turning grayish blue.

Alkali sucked in a deep breath. Exhaling slowly through his mouth, he felt a surprising sense of calm. His thinking cleared. He could hear his grampa's voice, just like he was talking to him. It was strange. It almost seemed like when they drove around together and discussed farming. Whenever the talk was about machinery and how it worked, Grampa would always end with the same lecture. The familiar words echoed in his brain, "Accidents are caused by carelessness, but it's panic that kills."

Alkali thought hard. "I can jump. I can get out. But Grampa—I can't leave him. Have to swing the combine away from the lake. First: get Grampa off the wheel."

Wedging his arm and shoulder between Grampa and the steering wheel, he braced himself.

"One—Two—Three! Humph!" Alkali grunted.

Grampa barely lifted off the column.

Then Alkali noticed Grampa's grip. His fingers were frozen on the wheel, white-knuckled, secure. Alkali concentrated his strength on prying off the stiff fingers. They were fast approaching the clump of bushes and tangled barbwire. Less than twenty feet and it would all be over. Alkali had to leap now or never.

Instead he braced himself and wedged in tight between the steering column and Grampa's belly.

"One—Two—Threeee—"

"Thump!" Alkali heaved Grampa back so hard that Grampa's head whacked the cab's rear window.

Alkali lunged and turned the steering wheel sharply, swinging the combine off course, up and away from the lake. The pickup table knocked off one of the rotting fence posts with such force that it flew over the cliff edge and splashed into the water below. Brush and broken strands of barbwire were fed into the combine's innards.

The machinery protested with a loud grinding and clang-
ing. Sluggishly, the combine moved through the bush and
then lumbered back up the slope into the golden stubble.

Before Alkali had a chance to even breathe a sigh of
relief, his attention was drawn back to Grampa, who
remained unconscious but gasping for air. Turning to the
sound, his eyes caught sight of the yellow button and the
red button. Until now Grampa's body had shielded the
controls on the right side of the cab. *Yellow button, ether—
to start the engine—could cause an explosion now. Red button, kill the engine. Right.*

Alkali lunged across Grampa's chest and punched
down the red button with his clenched fist. The forward
motion, the grinding gears—everything ceased instantly.
As the dust billowed past and the stillness followed, Alkali finally caught his breath. It was then that he realized for
sure that Grampa was still alive. He was no longer blue;
his chest heaved and fell with each struggling gasp.

Grabbing the CB mike, Alkali yelled, "HELP! SOME-
ONE HELP MY GRAMPA!"

Nothing. No noise. No static. Alkali banged the mike
against his hand. It stung but still nothing. Then he
remembered that he had turned it off earlier so it
wouldn't disturb Grampa. He reached up and turned on
the power switch. By now his disgust with his own panic
was more than he could take.

"HELP! PLEASE, SOMEONE HELP ME!"

Back at home base Mom heard the hysterical cry. She
hurried over to the radio. "52–29. This is home base. Do
you copy? Alkali—is that you?"

"Mom." He could barely talk. "Mom, it's . . . Grampa."

"Alkali, what's wrong?" Mom demanded.

"There's blood everywhere. He's sick." Alkali started to weep.

"Hold on, Alkali! I'm coming!" Mother called back.

Alkali dropped the mike and opened the door of the combine. The inrushing hot air quickly filled the air conditioned cab. It made him feel weak. He half-fell down the steel steps. When his feet touched the ground, he walked purposefully over to the scrub brush at the field's edge. He looked at the smooth surface of the lake and threw up.

CHAPTER
TWELVE

Alkali closed his eyes. It all came back to him. He could hear the ambulance attendant on the radio.

"Male, approximately seventy years of age. Unconscious. Airway open. Respiration: forty-four. Have commenced oxygen at five liters. Pulse: weak, rapid, a hundred plus. Blood pressure: unable to obtain. ETA: twelve minutes. Looks like a GI bleed. Call Cameron."

He saw the flashing red lights grow smaller as they disappeared in the direction of town. He could hear the siren wailing in the distance. *Why couldn't he go with them?*

"Alkali!" Dad called from the hallway. "Alkali!"

Roused from his thoughts, Alkali came to attention and swung his feet over the edge of his bed just as his dad walked into the bedroom.

"Your Mom just called. They took Grampa to Regina. He's in surgery now." Dad sat down on the bed beside him. The mattress sagged under his weight. Alkali felt as if he would slide onto the floor. He pushed back with his feet and shivered. Dressed in only his gotch, he scrambled to reach the comforter at the end of his bed. He cocooned himself in the quilting.

"Regina?" Alkali said. "Will he be all right?"

"I don't know," said Dad.

Clutching the quilt under his neck, Alkali picked up the sour smell of sickness from his hands. He had showered and soaped and scrubbed, yet the smell still lingered. It brought back the vivid memories: the red-orange vomit, Grampa gasping for air, the—

"See you got Timmy off to bed," Dad interrupted his thoughts. "It took a lot longer than I thought it would to clean the combine."

"Is Grampa going to die?" Alkali asked.

"They say he's critical."

"What does that mean?"

"It means—" Dad cleared his throat. "It means that Grampa is very sick." He turned away and looked out the window. "He's is in surgery to close up a hole in his stomach—to stop the bleeding. They say his lungs are congested, probably from when he choked. And his heart suffered. . ." His voice faded.

Alkali looked to see what his Dad was staring at. The yardlight shone on the little white bungalow across the yard. Grampa's house. Tonight it looked different. The house was dark, empty. Alkali could not ever remember seeing the house in darkness before. Always, Grampa left the porch light on, "In case someone came at night needing help."

"The doctor told Gramma that if he survives the surgery, the next twenty-four hours will tell the tale."

"I want to go see him now!" Alkali threw off the quilt and slid off the bed. He pulled open the bottom drawer of his dresser and grabbed a pair of blue jeans.

"Hold on." Dad reached for Alkali's arm and pulled

Alkali kicked the blue jeans off to the side and climbed into his bed. He tugged at the comforter and lay his head down on the pillow.

"Are you sure there isn't anything I can do?" Alkali asked as Dad turned out the light.

Dad walked over and gave him a kiss goodnight. Even after his dad was gone, Alkali could still feel the wetness of a fallen tear that was not his.

Alkali kicked the blue jeans off to the side and climbed into his bed. He tugged at the comforter and lay his head down on the pillow.

"Are you sure there isn't anything I can do?" Alkali asked as Dad turned out the light.

Dad walked over and gave him a kiss goodnight. Even after his dad was gone, Alkali could still feel the wetness of a fallen tear that was not his.

CHAPTER
THIRTEEN

Alkali woke up. He was surprised to wake up because that meant he had slept. He wondered for a moment if it had all been a nightmare: Grampa getting sick, the runaway combine, the ambulance taking Grampa away.

Then he heard unfamiliar voices. Women's voices. Lured by the sounds and smells of food cooking, he wandered down the hallway but stopped before entering the kitchen. Peeking around the corner, he saw Mrs. MacDonald and Margaret Begley. Both were hovering over Timmy as he sat at the kitchen table eating breakfast.

Suddenly embarrassed to be standing in only his undershorts, Alkali scurried back down the hallway to get dressed. He didn't want to think why they were there. He saw a pair of blue jeans in a heap on the floor. He remembered last night with Dad. As he slipped into the pants, he began to feel anxious. He returned to the kitchen entrance not knowing what to expect.

Timmy immediately spotted him.

"Everyone's come to help!" Timmy exclaimed.

It was true. The women had moved in to look after the boys and prepare meals for the men. The kitchen counter was covered with casseroles and baked goods. Mr. MacDonald and Mr. Begley were out swathing. The Dowler brothers had arrived with their grain trucks. Mr. Crane and Mr. Hyndman showed up with combines. All the neighbors had come to help.

"The twins are outside in the cave with the kittens!" Timmy continued almost shouting.

Alkali did not speak. It was all so confusing. Mrs. Begley came over and steered him to the kitchen table.

"Now, you sit yourself down. We've been waiting to make a hero's breakfast." She gave him a hug. "Oh, Alkali," she said, "I just can't help myself. I'm so proud of you."

"Me?" he asked, incredulous. He looked at Mrs. Begley and Mrs. MacDonald beaming down at him.

"How's Grampa? Has my mom called yet?" he asked.

"Your mom phoned earlier. Your dad took the call before he headed to the field," Margaret Begley explained as she pulled out a chair from the table for him. "He said so far, so good. Your mom and gramma are staying with Grampa. I think they expect your Uncle Craig to arrive in the late afternoon. Your mom will probably come home with him."

Alkali took his place at the table.

"Now, how about that breakfast?" Mrs. Begley asked. "Timmy wanted pancakes and bacon. What can we whip up for you?"

Alkali didn't say anything. He looked across the table at the mess of syrup and cakes. He didn't feel like eating.

"He just eats Shreddies!" Timmy said. "Everyday, the same thing, Shreddies with brown sugar!"

Alkali gave Timmy a look of irritation. "Twenty-four hours" played on his mind. Who could think of food!

"Grampa," Alkali said with great purpose. "He wants me to come."

The sun was shining brightly overhead when Dad stopped in to pick up lunch to take to the field.

"Come on in, Alkali. Out of the heat," Dad coaxed at Alkali who sat planted on the top step at the back door.

He just shook his head and scratched Fat Cat behind the ears.

"Alkali, what am I supposed to do? Beg?" Dad was exasperated.

"No," Alkali looked up into his dad's angry stare. "I told you. I want to go see Grampa."

"You know I can't just drop everything and drive to Regina!" Dad continued his way up past Alkali and into the house. The screen door slammed behind him.

Alkali felt bad for making Dad mad, but he knew he had to see Grampa. Soon.

He listened as his dad made excuses to the women in the kitchen. "The kid's upset. He and his grampa are— well, you know. . ."

Alkali heard the sound of chairs scraping on the floor and then the sound of something poured. There was the distinct tinkle of ice cubes against glass.

"Now, I'm not wanting to butt in—"

Alkali recognized Mrs. Begley's voice. He found himself smiling when he heard the part about butting in.

"But Jimmy, I think you should go to Regina. Take that boy and go see your father," she said.

Alkali cheered silently.

"I can't leave. How can I walk out when everyone is here to help?" Dad protested.

"That's exactly why we're here," Margaret Begley said. "The Dowlers can handle the trucking."

"And as for lunch," added Mrs. MacDonald, "Marg and I have taken our share of lunches to the field. We can manage quite fine. We'll take the small boys with us. They'll be delighted."

There was a silence. Alkali stopped stroking Fat Cat.

"Look at that boy." It was Mrs. Begley again. She was talking about him. "He's not eating. I got him to take a drink earlier this morning," she continued. "Why he even turned down my raspberry tarts. I don't remember anyone ever doing that before."

"He just mopes," said Mrs. MacDonald.

"He's worried sick. I say, take him to see his grandfather," Mrs. Begley interjected. "That's all he wants. He told us first thing this morning that his grampa wants him and he's still saying it."

"When Helen called this morning, she said that Dad keeps calling for Alkali," Jimmy said. "They keep telling him Alkali's fine. We just thought it was confusion. Alkali was with him when he got sick, so naturally when he came to, he was looking for Alkali."

When Alkali heard this, he jumped up and went to the door. He leaned with his face pushing against the screen mesh, peering at the adults sitting around the table.

"Well, then. . ." said Mrs. Begley.

"He wants me, Dad," said Alkali.

Dad looked over at the anxious face behind the screen. He sighed. "I guess it's settled. But there's no guarantee they'll let you into the Intensive Care," he cautioned.

Marg tapped her finger on the table. "Well, you just

make them. Now, let's get a lunch packed for the road."

The women scurried into action. "Timmy will stay with us. The twins will keep him busy."

"Alkali, come in and get cleaned up," Mrs. Begley ordered.

Alkali pushed Fat Cat away from the screen and opened the door. As he walked past his dad, he whispered, "Thanks." He continued to the bathroom.

Mrs. Begley was still giving orders. "Jimmy, you'll be able to meet Craig's plane. Make sure Helen gets some rest—Effie, too. And tell James we're praying for a speedy recovery."

CHAPTER
FOURTEEN

Gramma and Mom were surprised but delighted when Dad and Alkali walked into the hospital waiting room. It was just around three o'clock. The two women looked very tired. Alkali thought that Gramma looked older, which did nothing for his worry. And they were not allowed to see Grampa. The drive to Regina had taken almost two hours, and Alkali could not understand why he should have to wait. "Hospital rules," Mom explained. They were allowed to visit for five minutes every two hours, and they had just been in. The waiting room was filled with people looking sad and anxious. There was no place left where they could sit together, so they retreated to the hospital cafeteria for a snack and some privacy to exchange their news.

As they turned to leave the waiting room, Alkali saw the sign posted by a set of swinging doors. It said, "VISITORS PLEASE REPORT TO THE NURSING STATION" and below this, in smaller print it said, "No Children Under 12 Years Allowed."

Over coffee and pie—Alkali chose an ice cream bar— the women updated them on Grampa's condition. Alkali listened to their hushed voices. "The doctors said things could still go either way." Gramma talked about how confused he was and yet how strong. "The nurses say they're having real problems with him." Alkali wondered what that meant but felt he shouldn't ask now. He didn't eat much of his ice cream.

Dad told the news from home, how the neighbors had just moved in and everything was going so well, and how Timmy was in good hands. He even laughed when he told them about Marg Begley taking charge and telling everyone what to do. Gramma and Mom seemed a lot happier after hearing Dad's news. They talked about Uncle Craig, of how they should arrange their visits with Grampa, and they discussed the merits of Alkali seeing Grampa first. It was Gramma who insisted that he must. The adults decided on a game plan. No one consulted Alkali, but after hearing their plan, he didn't mind.

Uncle Craig's plane was to arrive at the same time Grampa could have visitors. Dad was to go to the airport to pick him up; Gramma would take Alkali in to see Grampa—if the doctors would give permission, and Mom would stay with them in the waiting room just in case.

Just in case what? Alkali wondered.

Leaving behind a melted ice cream bar, Alkali returned with his family to the Intensive Care waiting room. Dr. Abdullah was called. Together, the adults conferred. Alkali eavesdropped.

"We understand you have to have rules," Dad began. "But you see, doctor, the boy and his grandfather are very close." Dad held up his hand with two fingers crossed. "It was Alkali who was with him when he got sick. The boy saved his life."

Looking around the room, Alkali saw that the other people in the waiting room had heard it, too. They were staring at him. He felt embarrassed.

Dr. Abdullah nodded his head thoughtfully. Alkali thought it funny the way his family stood around the doctor, huddled like a football team.

"It might be helpful for Mr. Johnston also," said the doctor. "He has been calling out 'alkali,' but I am afraid we did not understand that 'alkali' was this young man, his grandson." The doctor paused. "We don't want to disrupt him, you understand."

Alkali flinched.

"But," the doctor continued, "I think an exception to the rule might be in order here." Dr. Abdullah motioned for Alkali to join the group.

Alkali felt even more conspicuous in front of the waiting room of strangers. The doctor placed his hand on Alkali's shoulder and then, eye to eye, said, "Young man, I have heard how you rescued your grandfather. I regard you with high esteem and respect. Now you must help your grandfather once again. He is very sick and is not himself as yet. I hope your visit will help calm him, help him orientate—help him understand where he is. We want him to settle down and get better. You will not need to talk, the less said the better. Do you understand?"

"I think so, sir," Alkali responded with uncertainty.

"Very well, I will arrange for your visit with the nursing staff," the doctor said. He turned to Dad and Gramma. "I want one of you to accompany the young man, please." Then he disappeared through the swinging doors.

Alkali stood wondering about the part about calming Grampa down. It seemed to Alkali that lately every time he was near Grampa, he just got the old man worked up. But how could he get out of it now?

"How much longer, Gramma?" Alkali asked.

"Not much longer, dear. The nurses just wanted a bit more time for some reason. They know we're waiting. They'll come for us soon," Gramma reassured him as she too watched the entrance to the Intensive Care Unit.

Alkali fidgeted on the plastic upholstered couch. It was uncomfortable. The waiting room was uncomfortable. The whole place was uncomfortable. There was nothing to do. Sure, they had an old television mounted in the corner, halfway up the wall, but the volume knob was broken and there was no sound. The picture was so poor that Alkali quickly discovered that it wasn't worth the effort to watch it. A stack of worn-out magazines looked uninviting. All that was left to do was watch people come and go. The people rarely smiled. Other families clustered together protectively and spoke in whispers. Some cried, especially after their visits through the swinging doors.

Alkali was starting to feel anxious. Maybe Grampa was calling for him because he was mad. He thought about the garden tractor and the tarp strap, Blacky, the kittens and all the trouble he'd caused. Maybe he should just stay away from Grampa.

"CODE 99—ICU. CODE 99—ICU. CODE 99—ICU," sounded over the hospital intercom. Alkali thought it strange. Up to now it had just called hospital people like "Dr. Kim, phone 369." Suddenly, men and women came running down the hallway. Some were dressed in white lab coats, others in what looked like green pajamas. They raced through the swinging doors of the Intensive Care. Alkali counted at least seven.

"Dr. Abdullah—ICU—STAT! Dr. Abdullah—ICU—STAT!" Alkali recognized him as Grampa's doctor as he bolted down the hallway and through the double doors.

"What's going on, Mom?" Alkali asked.

"I don't know, dear. There must be some kind of emergency," said Mom. She reached across to Gramma and held her hand.

Alkali looked at Gramma. She was weeping. With her free hand she dabbed at the corners of her eyes with a well-used Kleenex.

Alkali looked away. Was it Grampa? He looked at the other people sharing the waiting room. Their faces mirrored his fear. He *had* to see Grampa. Now. He stood up.

"Alkali, sit!" Mom scolded in a whisper. "All we can do is wait."

He plopped back down.

Mom reached over and clasped his hand. The Johnston's sat, holding hands, waiting. Everyone in the waiting room seemed paralyzed. No one moved. No one read. No one watched the television. They watched the wall clock. Seconds went by quickly, but it seemed that the minute hand barely moved.

Then Dr. Abdullah appeared through the swinging doors. Everyone looked at him.

Alkali could see that the doctor was not smiling. He looked very uneasy. The staff who had previously come running now exited from the ICU. Quietly, the white lab coats and green scrubs disappeared down the hallway.

"Mr. and Mrs. Drozda, may I have a word with you, please," Dr. Abdullah announced.

Alkali wanted to cheer. The bad news wasn't for them. "Grampa's okay!" he whispered to his mom. But Mom and Gramma were watching the couple who had been seated across the room get up. The man appeared to be holding the woman so she would not fall. Together, the couple and Dr. Abdullah walked a short distance down the hallway.

Alkali could hear parts of their hushed conversation, the woman weeping.

Alkali heard the sound of weeping beside him. It was Mom. And Gramma, too.

"Grampa's okay, isn't he?" Alkali demanded.

"For now, Alkali," Gramma answered. She sounded worn-out.

"Alkali," Mom said. "Those people just lost their son. He was in a car accident. They brought him in last night."

Alkali didn't know what to do. He just wanted to leave this place where so many people hurt. Just get Grampa and go home. Have things like they were. He didn't want to even think about life without his grampa.

A nurse poked her head through the double doors. "Mrs. Johnston. You can see your husband now." She disappeared behind the swinging doors so quickly that Alkali never really got a chance to see her.

Instantly, Mom and Gramma stopped their tears.

Gramma stood and smoothed her skirt. She patted her fingers around her eyes. "Helen, does it look like I've been crying?"

"I'm afraid so," Mom said.

Mom licked her index finger and tried to slick down Alkali's cow lick. It was impossible. The offending hairs remained down only momentarily, and at the first turn of his head, they sprang back to attention. Mom sighed.

"Okay, dear," said Gramma. "Let's go."

Alkali was surprised by Gramma's sudden change of mood. She seemed so calm. He felt reassured. Seeing Grampa was the right thing to do. He turned to Mom, who remained seated.

"What about you?"

"Only two visitors at a time," Mom reminded. "Grampa wants to see you, remember."

Together, they entered the Intensive Care Unit. It was like stepping into another world. The unfamiliar smell of Lysol and sickness made him feel faint. Only the coolness of the room saved him. As they approached the nursing station, one of the nurses looked up from her charting and gave a quick wave. Gramma nodded her head and kept going. Alkali could see they were approaching an area that was divided by glass walls and drapes. He heard bubbling sounds and then a sucking rattle. A steady succession of beeps grew louder. He saw beds at the center of each partitioned-off area. Each bed was surrounded by hospital stuff: bottles hung from the ceilings, tubes coiled down and around machines, minicomputers flashed red, and green lines danced across their screens. The only movement was a passing pink uniform. It took a moment, but then Alkali realized that in each bed, under layers of white, lay a very sick person, perhaps even a dying person. It suddenly made it all very real and frightening.

Alkali squeezed Gramma's hand. He was feeling weak and afraid. Just as he was preparing to turn and run, Gramma stopped. Sensing the turmoil in him, Gramma leaned over and spoke ever so gently.

"Your Grampa has always been there for you. Be brave, Alkali."

"Okay, Gramma," Alkali whispered.

A few steps further and they were standing hand in hand at the foot of Grampa's bed. He was very still, his eyes closed. The lower portion of his face was covered with a green oxygen mask. Underneath this, Alkali could see a tube protruding from one of Grampa's nostrils. It circled onto his chest like a coiled snake. It contained dark brown liquid. A plastic jar bubbled on the wall. Alkali leaned and looked at the little screen on the computer by the bed. Squiggly yellow-green lines hummed across without interruption. He glanced up at the bag of water hanging on a metal pole. A tube ran out the bottom of the bag. Alkali saw that it ended at Grampa's inner elbow under a gauze bandage. That's when Alkali saw something that disturbed him more than anything he had seen yet. Grampa's hand was tied down. Quickly glancing over Grampa's stomach, he saw that both Grampa's hands were secured with gauze ropes to the chrome bedrails.

Alkali was stunned.

"James? James. It's me, Effie. I have Alkali with me."

As Grampa opened his eyes, there was immediate recognition. Gramma leaned across the bed rails and delicately kissed Grampa's forehead.

Grampa struggled to lift himself off the bed that held him captive.

"Alkali."

Although the mask muffled the sound, it was still clear enough for them to hear. Grampa slumped back against the pillow in resignation.

Wanting to help, Alkali sprang to action and reached for the nearest gauze restraint. He fumbled as he tried to untie the tight knots.

"No, Alkali! You must not touch them!" Gramma spoke sharply.

"But Gramma," Alkali protested.

"No, dear. Grampa has to have them for now. Your Grampa has been very confused since the surgery; he keeps pulling out the tubes and tearing off the dressings. The doctor says it sometimes happens because of the anesthesia; that's the medicine they used to put Grampa to sleep for his operation."

Gramma turned to Grampa, "You're just too strong for them, aren't you, dear. And you just keep getting stronger."

Grampa looked directly into her eyes and nodded his head.

"Oh, James. You understand what I'm saying." Gramma pulled out the tissue she had tucked in her sweater cuff and dabbed her eyes.

Misconstruing Gramma's tears for grief, Alkali leaned down and placed his cheek against the only part of grampa that he could really touch—the back of Grampa's tied down hand.

"Don't die. Please, Grampa, don't die." Alkali started to weep. "You said you'd live to be a hundred."

"Alkali!" Again, the hoarse voice called from behind the oxygen mask.

Gramma, sensing Grampa's agitation, reached for the mask that covered his nose and mouth and loosened the elastic that held it in place.

Alkali let go of Grampa's hand and stood sniffing in an attempt to clear his nose. His fingers wiped away at the tears on his cheek.

"Alkali. I—" Grampa growled to clear his throat. "You —you did a good job on the chicken coop."

Alkali smiled. "Thank you, Grampa."

"You're a real James Johnston," Grampa said.

Alkali could see Grampa's eyes were starting to get watery.

"No," said Alkali, "I just want to be Alkali."

"Alkali," the old man repeated. "Grampa's Alkali." He nodded his head and his eyelids closed.

Gramma gently replaced the oxygen mask.

"Is he okay?" asked Alkali anxiously.

"Yes, dear. See his breathing? He's just sleeping. He needs his rest now if we want him to get better."

Alkali watched the rhythmic rise and fall of Grampa's chest. It looked right.

Gramma held out her hand to Alkali and together they walked toward the waiting room. As they passed through the swinging doors Alkali knew he would be back. He'd be back to take Grampa home.

ABOUT THE AUTHOR

Jo Bannatyne-Cugnet was born and raised in Estevan, Saskatchewan, and graduated with a degree in nursing from the University of Saskatchewan. She lives with her husband and four sons on a farm near Weyburn and still works part-time as a nursing supervisor though her time is increasingly devoted to writing books for children and young adults. She is the author of *A Prairie Alphabet*, an international best seller, and *Estelle and the Self-Esteem Machine*.